IN THEIR STARS

BY

WENDY HOWARD

IN THEIR STARS

Copyright 2022 Wendy Howard

And
Woodrow Publishing

****

This book is licensed for your personal enjoyment only. This book may not be re-sold, copied, or given away to others, unless in the original cover and with the permission of the author, Wendy Howard, or the publisher -

Woodrow Publishing
www.woodrowpublishing.com/

ISBN:9798424130823

DEDICATIONS

This book is dedicated to all the lovely people, friends, family and those new acquaintances who have supported and encouraged me to continue writing.

Thank you also to members of my family who have helped me with some of the story lines contained within these books.

This is the third book of this trilogy and so therefore the last, but who knows what might happen in the future?

WENDY

CONTENTS

CHAPTER 1 – JAMES	11
CHAPTER 2 – CAITLIN	28
CHAPTER 3 - A SURPRISE GIFT	56
CHAPTER 4 – AN AMAZING OFFER	68
CHAPTER 5 – THE GRAND OPENING	78
CHAPTER 6 -SURVIVING THE ELEMENTS	87
CHAPTER 7 - SUZIE	94
CHAPTER 8 - NEW LIFE – NEW CAREER	111
CHAPTER 9 – FUTURE PLANS	127
CHAPTER 10 - GOODBYE GRANDMA	138
CHAPTER 11 - A NEW GENERATION	143
CHAPTER 12 - MAISIE	148
CHAPTER 13 - HOME AND AWAY	159
CHAPTER 14 - SOUVENIRS OF KEFALOS	166
CHAPTER 15 - IMPORTANT DECISIONS	174
CHAPTER 16 – AN UNEXPECTED CALL	185
CHAPTER 17 - LAURA	191
CHAPTER 18 - AT SEASON'S END	196
CHAPTER 19 - IN THEIR STARS	201
MORE BOOKS IN THE TRILOGY	204

CHAPTER 1
JAMES

They had visited the island of Kos many times over the past few years, but this time it was different. Instead of the usual holiday flight during the season, on this occasion they were travelling via Athens, as direct flights to the island finished at the end of October and didn't recommence until April next.

Even though they had checked in several cases at Manchester Airport, they would not see them until they arrived on the island. This was a blessing, as each case was packed to capacity and weighed over twenty kilos each. They were now looking for the boarding gate for their short flight to Kos.

There had been much soul searching and a massive amount of organisation to get them to this point. It was also the biggest risk they'd ever taken, and they were anxious to see their plans coming to fruition.

The flight was short, around fifty minutes, hardly time from take off to landing for them to be served with a cold drink and have the empty glass collected before the plane began its descent into Kos. The weather was quite good for this time of year and there were only a few bumps on the runway, as they came into land.

They knew Nikos would be there to collect them, and as they didn't need to go through passport control because this was an internal flight, they passed quickly through the airport.

James took a deep breath, trying not to let anyone see how anxious he was feeling. He was hoping so much that he'd made the right decision, both for himself and for his family, however, only time would tell if his decision was right or wrong.

James was the second child of Jenny and John Peters. He had an older sister called Suzie, and a younger sister named Laura. He'd spent his childhood years living on the moors in a renovated farmhouse, where the family kept horses and dogs. As a young lad, James had many happy memories from his childhood, and looked back on them with great fondness. Now he was about to take the plunge and create a lot of new memories, but to take this step, he had to sort out some of the memories from his past life. The task before him was looming and he tried to concentrate, as there wasn't much time left to complete it. If he'd had more time it could have been quite pleasurable.

He remembered his younger sister Laura telling him how it took her ages to pack up her things when she moved to Kos, because each item took her on a path to her past and brought back memories, both happy and sad. Now he was doing the same, although his memory box was not as organised as Laura's had been.

James had thrown things untidily into boxes and drawers as his life took different turns. He hadn't really revisited them since he'd first put them away and now here he was, deep in the memories that each item took him to.

Karate Belts

He took a box from the top of the wardrobe. Inside this box was one of his karate belts, and he smiled to himself as he glanced at it. The memory was both an unhappy one, with flashes of bad situations and feelings that he'd let his parents down, but also one of accomplishment, when, by hard work and the help of his parents, he was victorious over his oppressors.

James had enjoyed school and had always done well, often being top of the class in most subjects and frequently winning class prizes for top marks and continued hard work.

Unfortunately this led him to be picked on by a group of boys in his class, who were jealous of his achievements. These boys dubbed him, 'teacher's pet,' and bullied him every day during break times, or as he left school for the journey home each day. They would twist his arm behind his back and demand money or possessions from him. They'd punch him and humiliate him as often as they could, making his life a misery.

For a long time he'd kept it a secret from his parents, hiding his bruised body and broken belongings from them as well as his inner feelings of despair, along with the constant worry of what these bullies might do next. When it finally came to light, his mother was horrified that children could be so cruel, especially at such an early age.

One day he came home from school and this time he couldn't hide his injuries. His eye was bloody and swollen and already turning black. His mother's shocked face was enough to make him confess to what had happened, and also the reason why he was always so hungry when he came home from school, as his lunch money had been snatched by the bullies.

His precious trainers had been trashed and his football shirt ripped to shreds. He cried himself to sleep at night, having had to lie to his mum and dad for all this time.

James made his mother Jenny promise not to go to his school, as it would only make matters worse for him. Jenny had told him she would have to let his father know, even though James pleaded with her not to. He thought Dad might think he was a bit of a wimp.

"Maybe I can come up with some kind of alternative," his mother suggested.

James felt relieved that everything was out in the open, but anxious as to how it could be resolved without further encounters with the bullies.

Jenny researched many of the anti-bullying sites, looking for suggestions that might help to resolve her son's situation. She knew that James had liked his school and had always done well, so she didn't really want to suggest him moving schools.

She finally came upon a possible solution when she enrolled James in the karate school in town, where he soon became an accomplished pupil gaining belt after belt, as he became more and more proficient at the sport. He began to attend competitions, winning medals and progressing to be a very talented and committed karate student. He avoided the bullies whenever he could, until he was totally ready to confront them.

A school lesson gave him a wonderful opportunity one day when the teacher told them that, in an upcoming English lesson, she would be asking them to give a presentation in front of the class. Each pupil was to give a short presentation to the class on their hobby, using any props they wished.

James spent a long time working out what he would say and how he would demonstrate the skills he'd learnt. He searched his cupboards for items he could use, putting them into a holdall. He practiced over and over again so as to get out the correct information and to be confident in his presentation techniques.

Many children gave talks on football, on brownies, on baking, on ice-skating and such pastimes. When it was James's turn, he set out the table in front of him with trophies and belts of various colours. He spoke enthusiastically about learning the art of karate, and with a smile on his face, told of the new moves which he'd learned and how he could use them if the situation arrived when he had to defend himself. He told the class just how much he could hurt his opponents if he needed to.

He explained that having these skills gave him the power, but it was a power to use wisely, rather than to use physical power against another. Although he was able to impart pain and suffering if he so wished, it was a deterrent to people when they knew this about him.

There was a lot of interest as he gave the presentation, and almost everyone clapped at the end of it. Funnily enough, after this presentation the bullies never bothered him, or attempted to hurt him again. Even funnier was the fact that each one suddenly wanted to be his friend. They were now afraid of James, lest he released his powers on them if they were still his enemy. He smiled inwardly each and every time they spoke to him in the future.

Football Trophies

In the box next to these karate trophies were a host of football medals, man of the match, players player, youth cup winners, along with a couple of match balls given to him when they'd finished at the top of the league.

James had been a keen sportsmen and football fan. He supported his local team and most Saturdays he went to the match with his father, John.

He started to play football at Junior School, soon becoming, 'the one you wanted on your team,' and was always picked first by whichever team captain who got to choose first.

He was naturally fast and accurate when passing the ball and also possessed a terrific shot, true and straight when shooting at the goal which made him a high scorer.

His height helped him react to the high balls, making him good at heading. He was a team player, and his fellow teammates liked him for this. He wasn't selfish in trying to score himself if one of his teammates was in a better position to pass the ball to.

He graduated to the local area Sunday League team, where he added to his collection of trophies.

One day whilst playing, he noticed that someone was watching him quite intently from pitch side. He forgot about the man viewing and got stuck into the match, playing skilfully and helping his team to win. When the game finally ended, after celebrating, James walked off the pitch. The gentleman, who'd been watching him specifically, approached.

"Hello Son, my name is Cyril Jones," the man introduced himself. "I hope you don't mind me speaking to you but I work with a youth team, which is a feeder team for Manchester City. I've been watching you play for a few weeks now and I'd like to invite you to come for a trial. How do you feel about that?" James was quite stunned by this invitation, as he hadn't planned on a career in football.

Mr. Jones explained that he would like to speak to James's parents, Jenny and John about this. James was given a telephone number should he wish to ring him and then he left.

In answer to his question, James wasn't sure how he felt about the invite. However, he loved playing football and this was a fantastic invitation. He would speak to his father about this and ask his advice.

The football scout, Cyril Jones came to see Jenny and John, and explained that the team he coached and trained, regularly played against other feeder teams for various clubs, and from these teams players were recruited for the youth teams of professional clubs. He stressed that mainly players from the club he coached went on to play for Manchester City, but only if they proved good enough and more importantly, committed enough.

James and his father listened intently, but the youngster said nothing. It would mean John or Jenny having to drive him to training sessions and to the home ground when matches would take place. They also left from the home stadium when playing away games.

"We realise that it would be a big commitment for all three of you, but we also assure you that it will not affect James's school work or attendance at his school," the scout assured them.

It truly was a great opportunity for James. He loved his football and John said it was up to the boy, but he would be prepared to support him by doing all the taxiing it would require.

It meant James would have to give up playing for his regular team but when he thought about it, it was every young players dream to be approached by scouts for professional clubs.

"I'll give it a try," he told Mr. Jones, even though in the back of his mind was the promise he'd made to himself to become a doctor.

A couple of weeks later he met the rest of the players and quickly became part of the team, playing in most of the games. Being a skilled and really talented player, he was soon respected by the other team members. The team trained hard and it took up much of his time.

Every weekend they travelled to, and played matches all over the county. Soon, it seemed James had little time for anything else. His school work seemed to suffer, even though he continued to be at the top end of the class with regards to exam results, he no longer held his customary position at the top of the ladder, Very soon, this began to worry him.

It was a hard decision for a young man, but it was a decision which he had to make to be true to himself. It was much more important to him to achieve the results he needed to go to medical school rather than spend all this time playing football. He discussed this with his father, and as usual, John was fully supportive of his decision to leave the game behind to continue with his preferred career option, to be a doctor.

Cyril Jones and his team tried to persuade him not to leave, but James had made his mind up. It was sad to say goodbye to the team because he would miss the camaraderie, but his future lay elsewhere.

He still went to watch the lads play whenever he could, and was thrilled to see that some of them actually went on to play for professional clubs.

As he smiled to himself, he thought this would be a good story to tell his children and grandchildren, that he was once offered a place with a top football team but it wasn't to be for him.

He heaved a huge sigh as he placed the trophies in the box. They were part of his life, but a part he'd left behind to pursue medicine, which was now giving him such a wonderful opportunity.

Photograph

In the drawer of his desk he found a creased envelope. When he opened it, he found a photograph of a new born baby. This took his breath away, as he remembered just who it was and why he'd kept it.

James remembered the excitement there'd been preparing for the new baby's arrival. All the family were involved in painting the bedroom and getting the crib down from the attic. His mother had been busy sewing new drapes for it. Boxes of baby clothes that had never been used were carefully washed, ironed and put in the drawers in a newly finished nursery.

His mother, Jenny, had related the stories of how he and his sister had been born and brought home to this house. How Suzie had been a Christmas present and soon after, James had been a welcome addition to the family. There had been a real sense of anticipation throughout the entire household. Even though they were only young, small children, they still shared the excitement with their parents.

James vaguely remembered the day when Mum went into hospital to have the baby; the day he was told he would be a 'Big Brother' and not the little baby anymore. He wasn't quite sure how he felt about that.

He and his sister were bustled off to their grandparents, where they usually enjoyed the special times they had with them. However today, Grandma did not seem to be her usual happy self. She always seemed to be talking in whispers or wiping her eyes.

Later in the day, when James's father came to pick up both he and Suzie, he sat them both, one on each knee, and tried to tell them the best way he could, that the baby they were so looking forward to meeting would not be coming home.

"But why?" asked James, but John could not find the words.

"Because the baby was so beautiful," Grandma said taking over. "God decided he wanted her to live with him in Heaven and become a shining star." Both the children looked a little bewildered.

They drove home in silence, sensing Dad didn't want to talk, and when they arrived home they found their mother sitting on her chair in the lounge. The two children rushed to her as she held out both her arms and they were all three engulfed in an embrace. She held back the tears as much as she could but eventually broke.

"Don't cry, Mum, she will be happy with God," Suzie quietly said to make her mother feel better.

Jenny had never been particularly religious, but she could see the two children were holding onto the idea that the baby had gone to Heaven to be a star, and that really gave her comfort.

Although their mother was emotionally drained, their father seemed to shutdown altogether. John always seemed to be angry and didn't want to play with them anymore. He shouted a lot and stamped around, so much so that they became a little frightened of him. Their mother didn't smile like she used to, and the atmosphere in the house was no longer its usual happy one.

This went on for quite a while, until one morning, they got out of bed to find Mum and Dad sitting together and actually smiling, in complete contrast from the way they had been.

"Come on you two, I have something to show you," Dad said, looking at them happily as he led them outside to the stables. "Something very special happened last night," he continued. "We were sent something wonderful to help us all. Look," he said.

A new foal had been born in the night, and their mother and father had fought to save it when it wasn't breathing after it had been born. Their relief when it finally began breathing properly was unbelievable, and it helped them address what had happened to their baby girl.

The foal was now standing, even though it was still a little wobbly. They watched the little thing feeding from its mother

"This is Star," John told them.

"Did Emily send it to us from Heaven?" asked James.

Dad looked at Mum and smiled. "I believe she did," he said, and now they all smiled. They had been reunited as a family by this new life.

James didn't really know what had caused the changes to his parents that day, he only knew he was so happy that life had returned to normal and they were indeed a family again.

As they grew older, James and Suzie were told about what really happened and how Emily had only been alive for such a short time, but they should never forget they had a sister who was never meant to stay on this earth, even though she was much wanted and loved.

That day, James had made the promise to become a doctor, a doctor who was so clever that children like Emily would never die.

He stared at the photograph for a few more seconds and then put it back in the envelope. He'd never forgotten that he had a sister, never ever, and it was this memory which had spurred him on, and this had given him a chance to honour another promise he'd made to his family.

When his mother had told him they were going to have another baby, James wasn't sure how to react. Again it would be nice not to be the baby of the family, but he was still anxious that what had happened to Emily could happen again, but perhaps this time it would be a boy and he would be stronger.

There was much joy when his younger sister, Laura was born and James became a perfect big brother to her.

He put the photo, old and tattered as it was from his constant handling, into the packing case.

Ouzo from Greece

Next he found an empty miniature bottle of ouzo, empty because he'd drank it as soon as it was given to him. Over the years he'd grown to love the taste of it. He also found some photographs his parents, taken on holiday in Greece.

When James was in his late teens, his mother and father announced to the family that they were going to go on holiday without the children for the first time since they'd been born. They were told by John and Jenny that they were going to a place called Kefalos, situated on the Greek island of Kos.

All three children were pleased for their parents. They had given them so many happy family holidays that they now deserved some quality time on their own.

"Mum, stop worrying, we will be okay," insisted Suzie when her mother was going over it again for perhaps the twentieth time, telling them what they had to do in the event of an emergency. They waved them goodbye as the taxi took them both to the airport.

James's thoughts turned to perhaps having a party whilst his parents were away, but then he remembered how a close friend had done this and the revellers and the gate crashers had wrecked his parents' house.

He thought about how he might stay out late at the weekend, but decided he needed every spare second to revise for college exams. Also in their absence it was up to James to feed and exercise the dogs whilst his sisters would share the tasks of looking after the horses. This would take up a big part of his spare time.

Being in charge of themselves made them realise how much work their parents did and how organised they were. It was hard work for the three of them, yet their parents normally breezed through all these things after they'd completed a full day at work. Perhaps they should appreciate their parents a lot more than they'd done previously.

The two weeks holiday passed very quickly. When their parents returned, they gushed about the wonderful place they'd found and how lovely the local people were. James noticed that his father was much more attentive to his mother, putting his arm around her, squeezing her hand and stroking her hair. They looked like they were in love again. It was obvious that they were very happy and had a fabulous holiday.

Jenny and John returned to Kefalos again later in the year, and their enthusiasm for the place never waned.

One particular occasion when they'd returned from a holiday to Kos brought a surprise announcement, when they told the family that they had decided to build a house in Kefalos and would make it their permanent home when they retired. However, in the meantime they would use it as a holiday home, as much and as often as possible.

The children were shown countless photos of the resort, the tavernas and the village, along with photos of the plot which they had purchased and the views it gave. They looked at the plans and could see how happy their parents were, they were absolutely thrilled with the project.

The Rose

James put the photographs away and felt for the remaining item in the drawer, a torn and bedraggled piece of tissue paper which held the remains of a rose with its petals, now discoloured and spoilt. Each child had been given a rose to keep in memory of their loved one.

It was a short time after building work on the house in Kefalos had commenced when James's father, John, had become ill. At first he just appeared tired, but they knew their father very well and he was usually an energetic and positive man. They noticed how his body had become frail, and how he was involving himself less and less in everyday tasks.

Visits and stays at the hospital became more frequent. They still tried to have family time but his father was easily exhausted, so it was a rollercoaster ride from day to day. The illness had ravaged his once athletic body.

On one particular evening he called the children to his room in the hospital. He told them how much he loved them all and how proud he was of each and every one of them.

When John knew his time was limited, he made Jenny promise to move to Kos and fulfil the dream they'd once shared. His last words to their mother were, she told all of them, "Whenever you feel sad or alone, look to the stars and I will be there for you."

James read the lesson at the funeral, faltering only a couple of times as he stood proudly next to his mother and holding her hand tightly to comfort her throughout the entire service.

The family grieved the passing of such a good man. He'd been a caring and loving father to his three children, as well as a wonderful husband to Jenny. They all knew how much he'd loved them and were thankful for such a good role model and teacher.

Things slowly began to return to some sort of reality. There were good days and bad days for each of them. A familiar song would bring tears, a favourite cap hung on the peg, even the dogs wandered around in a daze appearing to look for him. They all missed him so much.

James had tried to persuade his mother not to move to Kefalos alone but she'd insisted on going, saying she must carry out her husband's dying wish. She knew she was taking John with her in her heart and a few months later, Jenny left for her new life in Kefalos, although sadly alone.

College Days

Something had gone down the back of the drawer and James tugged to retrieve it. He found it was his college scarf, a scarf he'd once been so proud to own. He had applied himself to his studies wholeheartedly. If he was to secure a place at medical school he needed to excel in the science subjects, along with maths and English.

His parents had been told by his tutors that he was well on course to achieve straight 'A's' across the board, and James expected nothing less, given the hard graft he'd put in. Suffice to say he achieved everything, just as he'd anticipated.

His interview for medical school went well. He'd done his research and was able to answer all the questions with good knowledge of the subject matter. He could also show true understanding of each topic covered.

A few weeks, later he received an invitation to attend the medical school of his choice. He prepared to leave home and move into shared student accommodation close to the college. On his first day he felt excited with anticipation, as this was the first step on his career path, the career he had promised to follow when his tiny baby sister had died all those years ago.

His thirst for knowledge was unyielding. He attended the lectures, took copious amounts of notes and then researched the topics online to fill any gaps that might be there. Some of his fellow students thought he was a bit of a nerd, as he spent very little time on the normal college leisure activities, although he did join the college football team, where his skills were very much appreciated.

The scarf was the last item which was personal to just him, as other mementos of his life so far had been kept elsewhere. His trip down memory lane was over now.

He really did have to get a move on now and continued to pack and box things up. It was tiring, especially after a hard day's work, and that evening he sat back in the chair and soon fell into a fitful slumber.

It must have been seeing the scarf, for in his dreams he returned to his college days and thought how lucky he'd been to meet Caitlin there, the girl who would become his life partner. He'd admired Caitlin from a distance. She always questioned everything during lectures and practical sessions, and always wanted to leave no stone unturned in gaining the knowledge and skills to be a true professional in her sphere of work.

James watched how she smiled when she worked out a problem, or fully understood what was being said to her. Her thirst for perfection inspired him. A couple of times she smiled at him across the lecture theatre and he wondered what was going through her mind.

One day in the refectory hall he sat with his book and lecture notes piled high, trying to read whilst having a sandwich for his lunch. He felt a tap on his shoulder and turned to see it was Caitlin.

"Hi," she said and smiled. "Is it okay for me to join you? If you're not too busy, I'd like to tap into your knowledge about a subject we covered last week."

James had just taken a bite of his sandwich before she spoke to him, so he nodded nervously and gestured for her to sit down at the table with him. Gulping down the last morsels, he smiled at Caitlin and said, "Of course." As she smiled back, he noticed how her eyes sparkled when she smiled.

James had always been quite a confident teenager and his results and acceptance into medical school had certainly helped, but sitting so close to Caitlin, he became a little tongue tied for some reason.

"So how can I help you? Which lecture did you want to discuss?" James questioned.

"To be honest, there isn't anything really," Caitlin smiled, looking him straight in the eyes. "I just wanted to talk to you," she continued. "You always seem so intense when we're in lectures listening to the tutors or learning something new, so I haven't wanted to interrupt." Hearing this, James smiled back at her, his delight at what she'd just said could not be contained.

"Coffee?" he asked.

"Yes please, with plenty of milk and sugar," she replied.

As he walked back, James noticed his hand was shaking carrying the coffee. Was this shaking caused by nervousness or excitement at meeting this lovely girl?

Caitlin smiled as he returned to his seat. Again, James thought how lovely she was when she smiled. Luckily she smiled a lot, and that gave him a really warm feeling inside.

This was the beginning of a relationship that developed all through their years at medical school.

CHAPTER 2
CAITLIN

Caitlin told James all about herself, how she'd discovered in her teenage years that she'd been adopted. She'd always wondered why her parents were so much older than those of her friends and schoolmates. Although she'd had a fairly normal childhood, she was always taught that hard work and commitment led to success, and had therefore been made to study hard at school, which led to a somewhat sheltered life outside of it.

She didn't go out at night like her friends, nor did she have boyfriends. She was never encouraged to invite friends to her home, and as a result of this she wasn't asked to others homes. She missed out on girly times like sleepovers, and on gossip in general. Because of this she became a loner, and was more and more ignored by her acquaintances. She made good use of the extra time she had by excelling at school and getting excellent results across the board.

Her parents were active in the church community and charity organisations, so Caitlin learned at an early age about poverty and the abuse of children who were far less lucky than she was.

Sadly, Caitlin was to have a fairly loveless relationship with her adoptive parents. They looked after her well, but there were no hugs or kisses from either parent.

While she was a teenager, her adoptive parents brought another girl into the household. This new girl had been neglected and abused, so she'd been taken in by social services for her own safety. She was a frail little thing, always with a runny nose! No matter how much time was spent combing her hair, she always looked unkempt. Caitlin enjoyed the company of the little girl and tried to help her with her schoolwork.

One day little Tracy became sick, but no one seemed to know why. She was lethargic and her head seemed to be too heavy for her shoulders to hold up. The doctor was sent for and he immediately called for an ambulance. He recommended that the house be disinfected and that Caitlin went to stay elsewhere for a few days but there was nowhere else for her to go, so she sat it out at the house whilst her parents spent long days and nights at the hospital.

Caitlin heard them whisper the word, "meningitis," but she wasn't sure what that was. Tracy became desperately ill and there was nothing to be done when the disease ravaged her already frail body.

"Why can't someone do something to help her?" Caitlin heard her adoptive mother say. "These doctors don't know anything."

Sadly but not unexpectedly, a few days later, Tracy passed away. Caitlin decided that day that she would become a doctor, but a doctor who 'did' know something, a doctor who could help sick children like Tracy.

A few years later her adoptive father died, followed a short time later by her adoptive mother. The church community rallied round her, and helped by the money from her adoptive parents wills, she was able to cope alone.

Her acceptance to medical school had been a dream come true. She worked hard on her studies each day so that she would become a doctor as she'd promised herself. She obtained a flat in the area close to the medical school and began to live alone and independently.

On the course she saw James. She kept looking at him but he was always so intense. She spotted him in the refectory during one lunch time and, pulling all her resolve together, she spoke to him. This was something which she'd never regretted doing, as with James, she'd found love and real friendship for the first time in her life.

They studied hard together, both knowing what they wanted to achieve. They compared notes and challenged each other's perception and understanding of things, but best of all, they were inseparable.

When James planned to go to see his mother, he asked Caitlin to go with him. She'd never been to Greece before but James had explained all about his mother moving there when his father had died, so how could the girl refuse him?

Kefalos

Jenny had been living in Kefalos for a little while when James and Caitlin went to visit her. The flight was quite smooth with very little turbulence. As they began the final descent into Kos airport, he became quite emotional at the thought of seeing his mother again. Okay, they often talked and could see each other on Face-time, but it wasn't the same as seeing his mother and being able to hug and kiss her properly.

As they passed through passport control, James scanned the waiting people in the arrivals lounge. Eventually he caught sight of his mother and pushed his way through to greet her. He thought how well she looked, and so young. Her holiday tan really suited her and it took years off. No longer did she look like the fragile, weather worn woman he'd taken to the airport for her journey to start her new life here on the island of Kos.

He made an excuse for the tears that filled his eyes as he hugged his mum for the first time in ages. Caitlin remained in the background during this precious reunion, but now she stepped forward and James introduced her to his mother. Jenny could tell instantly how much this young woman meant to her son. She could see it in his eyes, which were so much like his father's eyes.

James made the error so many do when first arriving in Kos when he went to the driver's door instead of the passenger side.

"Are you driving, dear?" Jenny asked, causing much laughter.

As they had a twenty minute drive from the airport to Kefalos, Jenny pointed out places of interest during the journey. She showed them the various beaches and the volcanic island of Nissyros, which was today bathed in cloud.

As they rounded the large bend on the approach to the Bay of Kamari, Jenny pointed out Kastri Island and explained how many people were married there. James was mesmerised by the scenery. It really pleased him that he could hear from his mother's voice just how much she loved Kefalos, and how happy she was to live here.

Although he'd seen the plans and many photos of his parents' house, he was overcome by the location of the property, perched high on the hillside with panoramic views of the entire bay, with beautiful gardens surrounding the house. He carried the heavy cases up the outside staircase to the front door of the house, which was built with a basement beneath it.

Jenny gave them a guided tour of the house and then asked if they would be okay together in the black and white room. He could tell that his mother was a little unsure when offering them a room together and he loved her for it. The room was beautiful, and James could see that Caitlin was also delighted with the room.

Jenny left them alone and went to make them each a frappe whilst they unpacked. After this, they went to sit outside on one of the many balconies, where they chatted together for hours.

During their stay, Jenny took them to various beaches to show the difference from one side of the island to the other. Kochylari on one side was blessed with wonderful breakers and warmer sea temperatures, whilst the bay of Kamari, being horseshoe shaped, was quite calm most of the time, with the sea being colder. The Greeks always said this was because fresh water streams filtered into the sea there.

Jenny took them to Kos town despite telling them, "I only come here when I really have to," and that she was always glad to get back to the tranquillity of her home in Kefalos.

They bought a few items from the many tourist shops running from the main square, and then went down to the marina to look at the fantastic boats and yachts moored there. This was a bustling town, not at all like the quiet calm of Kefalos.

Jenny, continuing to be their tour guide, took them to Plaka, which was also known as the hidden or sunken forest. The road down to Plaka was just past the airport, a rocky road with deep troughs caused by water flow following the rains.

After crossing over a little bridge, they came to a parking area. They could already see several of the Peacocks which lived there, some with young chicks scurrying behind them. Unfortunately Plaka had also become a place where people abandoned unwanted cats and kittens, resulting in the entire area being overrun now with cats, and people now came to feed both them and the peacocks.

The trees formed a canopy over the road and it was a little frightening when the daylight went at the end of the day, with the trees casting strange and frightening shadows. It was a well known fact that sometimes gypsies would camp under these trees.

James and Caitlin were intrigued with where Jenny was taking them. The road seemed to go on forever. They drove through the village, past the school and continued past the road that led down to the harbour. This road twisted and turned, but offered fabulous views of the harbour.

At a crossroads they bared to the right, where the road went on past farmland and they noticed large properties were scattered on the hillside. They came to a small stall, so Jenny pulled up and they got out of the car to purchase honey from the vendor.

"The thyme honey in Kos is very popular with tourists," Jenny informed the two. "The Greeks would tell you it's the best in the world."

When they returned to the car, the journey took them past churches and remote houses. Jenny began to slow down. James and Caitlin peered out of the window to see why his mother had come to a stop in the middle of the road. They spotted a large herd of multi-coloured goats wearing jingling bells, all strolling down the road and blocking it completely. The goats hurried a little when the car had approached but had now returned to a leisurely pace, choosing to stop and nibble at the vegetation as they passed. When they were ready they all left the road and continued into the gorse covered landscape. Jenny began to edge forward until the last of the goats had left the road and the three could continue their journey.

There were signposts now to various beaches, but Jenny remained on the road and eventually they came to a wide turn. There before them was a spectacular view of the sea, with superb waves dancing on the surface.

There was a restaurant overlooking the Bay and Jenny pulled up outside. She knew the owner and he was pleased to see her as she introduced her son and his girlfriend to him. They ordered drinks and sat mesmerised by the continuing rollers in the bay.

After refreshments they took a little walk along a sandy track which brought them out near a little church. Jenny explained that each time she came here she lit a candle in memory of John, her first husband and James's father.

"Your father often brought me here," Jenny divulged. "And now, every time I pass, I stop and light a candle in his memory." James and Caitlin joined in this tradition and lit a candle each.

Jenny took them further along a sandy road which led to several rocky inlets, which although not easy, you could scramble down to the sandy beach below. She told them how the way this landscape dropped steeply to the sea reminded her of her holidays in Cornwall.

It was obvious that the pair wanted to relax now on a beach, so Jenny drove them back and took them to Kochylari, which had become their favourite. She left them there and told them she would pick them up later, allowing them time on their own to take in the magic of this beautiful beach.

The two of them walked hand in hand on the sand and very soon they'd walked the entire length of the beach. They didn't speak but walked in silence, just taking in the total peace and tranquillity of this magical place. The waves were uncharacteristically small today, lapping ashore rather than crashing as they normally did.

"I could easily live here," Caitlin said breaking the silence. "This is as near to perfect that I can imagine. Maybe we will get a chance to retire here one day, but many years from now."

Hearing Caitlin saying this, made James smile. He felt exactly the same about Kefalos and its beautiful beaches, quaint streets, its friendly locals, and of course the beautiful sunshine and mild climate. Life always felt better when the sun was shining.

Some evenings they ate out in the many tavernas down in the resort area and sometimes Jenny cooked for them at the house, introducing them to many traditional Greek dishes.

They sat on the balcony chatting until late in the evening, relishing each and every second of the time they were given to spend with each other. They talked about their memories of James's father and laughed at the antics they'd shared. Caitlin had never had family time like this, but she thoroughly enjoyed having the stories recounted to her.

All too soon it was time for them to leave. James was extremely sad to say goodbye to his mother, although he felt relieved to see how well she was looking and how settled she was here.

"Mum, I believe both Caitlin and I have also fallen in love with this place you call home," her son told Jenny, promising to return to Kefalos just as soon as possible.

Laura's Graduation

A few months later, James received a telephone call from his younger sister, Laura. She told him how she was being presented with a special award from University and wanted him to come to the ceremony.

"Please bring Caitlin with you," Laura said.

James was delighted that his sister had done so well. He knew that, unlike himself, who found learning easy and didn't have to put in much effort, Laura had worked tirelessly at University to be successful as she wanted her parents to be proud of her, especially her father, John.

She went on to tell James that she'd spoken to Mum and had invited her.

"Of course I will come, my darling," Jenny had said, but then her mother had asked if she could bring someone with her. Laura and James both laughed and placed bets about who it would be and what they would look like. Dates were written in diaries and arrangements made for the family get together.

When James and Caitlin arrived at Laura's flat on the day of the presentation, Suzie was there with her husband, Daniel. He noticed his mother; Jenny was already there, with a handsome dark haired Greek man accompanying her.

"I see Laura won the bet about the looks," James announced as he was introduced to Yiannis, his mother's companion.

Although he didn't realise it, he began to rapidly question Mum's 'friend' about himself and his intentions regarding his mother.

"I intend to marry your mother," Yiannis revealed with honesty, also revealing he was totally in love and besotted with her.

Yiannis also told James that he owed Jenny a great debt, as she'd saved him from drowning in a remote cove on the island of Kos.

"Like your mother with your father, I had also lost my wife and was devastated," Yiannis said, just about stopping the tears from flowing. "But your mum, Jenny, taught me to love again."

James soon came to realise how much this man loved his mother, and that obviously she was also very fond of him. He instantly liked the guy and it was the beginning of a good relationship.

It would only be a short time before he would be travelling to Kos to attend the marriage, and to be honest, he genuinely felt privileged to have been asked to give his mother away at the ceremony.

Jenny's Wedding

The wedding took place in the tiny church positioned on the island of Kastri. It was a beautiful and romantic setting. James was very proud to stand next to his mother at the ceremony, knowing how much she had loved his father, and how she'd now found love again with Yiannis. Although uncertain at first, James was now happy with this relationship.

Once they were all back on dry land in the harbour, a horse and carriage took his mother and Yiannis to the restaurant where the reception was to be held. It was a wonderful occasion and the whole family were happy that love had finally found its way back into the lives of these two lovely people.

Laura, James's younger sister, left soon after the ceremony as she had big commitments back in England, but James and Caitlin and his older sister, Suzie and her husband, Daniel, remained for a further week.

Relaxing after all the excitement of the wedding, they lazed in the sun on the various beaches which they'd come to love, all agreeing their favourite was Kochylari, with its endless stretch of sand and constant waves breaking onto the shore.

When the time came for them to return to England, more than a little sadness filled their hearts, not just because they were saying goodbye to Mum for a while, but also because they were leaving a place they'd learned to love deeply, both for its natural beauty and also for the friendliness of the local inhabitants of Kefalos who remembered them from their previous visit and made them feel extra special.

Working Together

Following the wedding and the tranquillity of Kefalos, James and Caitlin returned to their frantic pace of life, working side by side at the hospital.

One day, when a small child was admitted as an emergency, both James and Caitlin responded to the call. The seemingly lifeless and limp body of the tiny child was lying on the much too big for her operating table. The medical staff on duty looked at each other and all came to the same conclusion, there was little they could do for this very sick child. However, James and Caitlin both made the same decision simultaneously and began shouting instructions to the rest of the medical staff in the room.

Drips were attached and CPU was administered, with the child's hands and feet being rubbed to encourage circulation. The child gave a little whimper and momentarily opened her eyes. Her chest rose and fell and she began to breathe

"That's for Emily," James whispered

"That's for Tracy," Caitlin mouthed.

They both knew why they continued to give all they had to the job, and all their hard work had been rewarded. All the study and learning they'd endured was worth every moment, just to be able to save the life of this small child.

Caitlin's Quest

Caitlin had always wondered about her birth mother. Her upbringing by her adoptive parents had been strict, with a heavy leaning towards religion.

Following their deaths she let her visits to the church slip, as she'd never felt completely right with the dogmatic approach of the religious institution. Medical School had been her religion, ever since giving every hour she had to learning the skills she hoped would provide her with a sound career within paediatric care.

Now that she and James were living together and talking about marriage with the possibility of children she decided it might be a good time to try and find her birth mother, but wasn't sure where to begin.

She found a few helpful articles online, as well as being able to research alternative avenues in the library. She wondered if amongst the papers and documents which her parents had left, there could be any vital clues.

She'd never looked inside the sealed boxes which she'd brought from her parents' house, after it had been sold following their deaths, and she'd kept the boxes on the top of the wardrobe for a few years now.

James was on a long shift today, so she was alone in the flat. She lifted the first box down and broke the seal. Inside she found many documents relating to her parents church activities, an old hymn book and a couple of battered prayer books, one with a small leaflet inside showing it was given to her adoptive mother at her confirmation ceremony, presided over by the Bishop. These didn't really relate to her at all, so she reached for the second box.

Inside this box, she found it contained a little more information about her, as it held details of her christening and confirmation at the age of eleven. Along with this there were also several certificates for regular attendance at Sunday school, school reports and class prizes.

It touched Caitlin a little that they'd kept all these, as they'd never shown any real pride in her achievements and took no responsibility for them. They always brushed off any praise by saying they were just doing what God had told them to do. She closed the box, now knowing it contained nothing inside which really helped her.

Inside the third box, amongst copies and pieces of paper was a small briefcase type file which had a lock on it. Caitlin wondered what she might find inside, should she could manage to unlock it.

The lock looked a lot like the ones you could buy from the pound shop, where many of the keys supplied fitted every lock. After searching she managed to find a few such locks, all with their tiny keys still attached. She tried each key in the lock of the briefcase until one finally opened it. She hoped it was worth the time and trouble taken, as she took out a cardboard file from inside.

Here she found a document relating to her adoption, showing the date it was finalised and the names of her adoptive parents, but sadly nothing before her actual adoption information. It showed it had all been arranged through the church, as many adoptions were in those days, when there were unmarried mothers. Caitlin wondered if this was the case regarding her own birth mother. She continued to wade through the documents, but found nothing else of any importance.

She thought about the next step she could take on her quest for information, finally deciding to go to the church where she'd spent so many hours, to see if the priest there could tell her anything.

She put everything away except for the adoption papers, which were dated and stamped as an official document. Perhaps she could trace something with this. She rang the priest and arranged to meet him in a couple of days.

It was strange to go back to the village where she'd grown up with her adoptive parents. Many houses had been built since her last visit, even the school playground had been updated by removing the old items, since they were now deemed as unsafe for young children.

She smiled to herself, reminiscing about the many times she'd visited and played in there without accident or any thought of danger. She remembered how she used to be swinging on the parallel bars, or twirling round on the swings without any fear for her life!

She knocked on the door of the priest house. A man answered the door but it wasn't the priest who'd been there when she was young. She then remembered he was an old man even then, so realised it could not possibly be the same priest after all this time.

"You must be Caitlin," he smiled. "I am Father John. Please come into the study," he invited, ushering her inside. "Now, what can I help you with?"

"I'm trying to find my birth mother, Father," she said to the priest, and went on to explain how she'd been adopted when a very young child, with the adoption being arranged through the church.

"My adoptive parents were both heavily involved with this church and I was wondering if there were any records available about my adoption," she told the priest. She continued to tell him about her life now as a paediatric doctor and having met a nice guy.

"We are planning to get married and start a family of our own," Caitlin confided to Father John. "This is why I really want to find my real birth mother."

The priest explained that a lot of adoptions carried by the church had been called 'closed files' to protect the privacy of the mother giving her child up for adoption.

"However, some laws have changed, meaning some files are now available to the public," the priest revealed seeing her disappointment. "I'm not sure how far back these files go, or what records we still have on file, but we can certainly take a look for you."

He asked Caitlin for her date of birth and looked at the adoption paperwork which she'd brought with her, but unfortunately there was very limited information on the document.

"I will speak to the parishioners and see if any of them remember anything. Maybe they can help," he said. "I will contact you if anything comes up."

"You promise, Father?" Caitlin requested, almost pleading.

"Of course I will, Caitlin," the priest smiled.

"Thank you Father," she smiled in return. "Thank you so much."

She walked down the lane to the church itself, where she wandered into the churchyard and searched for the grave of her adoptive parents. The last time she'd visited here, the graves were just soil piled high, allowing it to settle before a gravestone was added.

She eventually found the site and saw that a black head stone with gold lettering had been erected. It showed her adoptive father's name first, with the date of his passing, and then the details of her adoptive mother, but what was underneath at the bottom of the head stone shocked Caitlin.

'Baby born sleeping,' it read, but there was no further information, no name or date. She wondered why and suddenly felt a shiver run through her body.

She'd never known that her adoptive parents had had a child, for they always said that they weren't able to have children and that God had led them to her to be their child, as he had with Tracy.

Finding this piece of information added even more fuel to her chosen career in paediatrics. There and then she vowed yet again that she would do it for Tracy and for this young unnamed child.

She began to think that it was a bit of a wild goose chase, trying to find out about her birth parents, so she stopped thinking about it and got on with her busy life at the hospital. It therefore came as a total surprise when, a few months later, she received a package through the post. There was a handwritten letter with it from Father John, the priest she'd visited that day.

It went on to say:-

'Madam

We found this envelope in the archives and as it is addressed to you, we have not opened it. I hope this gives you some of the answers you are searching for.'

Caitlin's hands began to shake as she tried to unseal the large envelope. A tiny bracelet made of ribbon fell out. It said, 'Baby,' but with no name, although it did include the date of birth and the baby's weight. Was this her?

She emptied the total contents of the envelope out on the bed beside her, and with trembling fingers she picked up the document, a birth certificate. The mothers name was not properly legible and it showed the father as, 'deceased.' Although Caitlin recognised the date as her birthday, the child's name had not been added.

There were a couple of badly faded photos of a tiny newborn baby, and then one of a toddler. Was this really her?

Finally she came to the last paper item in the large envelope, a smaller sealed envelope covered with kisses on the sealed part. She carefully opened it to discover that inside it contained a handwritten letter.

She looked at it with a great deal of trepidation. Did she want to read this? Butterflies filled her stomach. Did she really want to know if this was about her and her birth mother? The tension was immense. She held the letter next to her chest and prayed for the first time in years, after which, she decided she had to read the letter.

It read:-

'To my darling daughter,'

She had never ever heard any terms of endearment from her adoptive parents, although she'd been well cared for by them, it was their love of God that she'd been frequently told about. It was so hard for her to read this letter, and soon tears began appearing in her eyes. Oh how she would have loved to have heard this said to her.

She began reading the letter again -

'To my darling daughter
I really hope that it's my little girl reading this. I wrote this letter just for you because I wanted you to know how much you were wanted. The truth is that I loved you from the moment I

knew I was expecting you. Your father and I were so excited that we were to have a child, and planned so many things for you whilst you were growing in my body. When you were born, I couldn't take my eyes off you.

It was the most difficult decision I have ever had to make to agree to your adoption. Although my parents had brought me up well, and I did love them, I haven't spoken to them since my marriage to your father.

I often wondered what sort of childhood you had, and always hoped it was a happy one. I myself had a happy childhood and my parents made sure my life was full of joyous occasions. It was only when I introduced your father to them and they discovered he was not Jewish that they tried to persuade me to forget about him and marry another boy from the same faith as them, a good Jewish boy.

For the first time in my life, I was not in agreement with my parents. I was so in love with your father that I went against their wishes and married him. It was easier for me to move away than to see the disappointed looks and hurt on their faces, so we moved to England and were married there.

Your father and I hadn't been married very long when I found out I was expecting you. At that time we rented a small flat, and everything in our lives seemed perfect. I was overjoyed at the thought of having a baby and we planned many things for you, but then my world fell apart.

Your father, whom I loved very much, was killed in an accident the month before you were born. He never got to meet you and I know he would have loved you as much as I do.

Suddenly I was on my own, expecting a baby and without a penny to my name. I couldn't ask my parents for help, as they didn't approve of my husband. They were orthodox Jews and very proud people, and because your father was not the same faith, they would not accept him. When he died I was left destitute, not knowing which way to turn.

As I carried you, I tried over and over again to find a way for us to be together, but I was young and pregnant with no prospects of finding work or any income. I was friends with a young girl in the village and she told me about how the church helped unmarried mothers. I told her I was married, but was now a widow. Mary said that as I was still young, she was sure they would help me.

I spoke to several of the Church council who seemed to understand my situation and they took pity on me. One of them even offered me work after the baby was born, but I had no one who could take care of you if I worked.

These people were very nice and told me they would find a good home for you. I didn't want to give you away but I had nothing, not a penny to my name.

It was terrible saying goodbye to you, and I will never forget that day as long as I live. You lay wrapped in the blankets I had knitted whilst alone in the flat waiting for you to arrive. I gazed at you and felt nothing but love. You gurgled and opened your big eyes and looked straight at me.

'Yes I am your mummy,' I thought to myself, with my heart breaking. I knew that I would never get to hear you call me that.

The midwife allowed me one last cuddle before they took you away. You would have a new family, a new mum and dad. As she carried you from the room, I cried myself to sleep.

Even though my mother and father were no longer part of my life, I want you to know about your grandfather. He was a great man and I was told about what had happened to him when I was a young girl.

In the later years of World War Two, your grandfather was taken from Krakow and was transported by a cattle truck to the camp at Auschwitz, along with many others from his village. Although he managed to survive the long journey, standing all the way in the carriage, he survived because he managed to position himself near a gap in the wooden door and so had access to air. Sadly, because of lack of air, food and water, several passengers did not survive the journey.

He arrived at Auschwitz Birkenau in the dead of night and could see tall chimneys spewing out flames and ashes from the fires of the crematoria. The ashes were falling like snow!

The doors of the carriages were opened and the occupants were met by snarling dogs, guards in SS uniform, and scrawny looking men wearing what looked like striped pyjamas. Those who were a little slow were hit with large sticks to hurry them on their way.

"Men in this line and women and children in this line," an officer shouted in German.

At the time your grandfather was a young strong man, so he was chosen to work. Little did he know that many of his fellow villagers were led directly to the gas chambers and died that day!

My father, your grandfather, had been studying at medical school and was near finishing and graduating as a doctor, so when questioned about the work he'd done, he said he was a qualified doctor. It was this little white lie he'd told which probably saved his life. He was put to work in the camp hospital, where he witnessed many horrific sights which he would rarely speak about.

He told me a little about his time in Auschwitz and how distressing it was. When the camp was liberated at the end of the war, he was only half the weight he'd been when he arrived at Auschwitz Birkenau. He bore mental scars so deep, because of what he'd seen and suffered during his time there. He showed me the number which had been tattooed on his arm upon arrival that night, but he did so as if he was ashamed of it.

He met and married my mother when he was still quite young. With her care, patience and love, he slowly returned to health and regained his strength. However, for the rest of his life he was forever plagued by horrific nightmares about the place he'd lived, if you could call it living.

I later heard from other people who told me that during his incarceration he'd helped to save many people in the camp. He was a hero, yet he told me so little about it.

I believe you would be very proud of your grandfather. Even though I had a disagreement with him about the man I married, he was still a great man, with strong principles.

He told me I should be true to my Jewish heritage because there were so few remaining Jews alive after Hitler's holocaust. I was proud of my father, and if you could have met him, I'm sure you would have been proud of him too.

My darling girl, I'm sure your adoptive parents will have loved you, just as I still do. I wish you happiness and success in your life, and I am so sorry that I could not be a part of it.

I loved you then and I love you now. I will always love you,

Mum x x

Caitlin was overcome with emotion. She was amazed and couldn't believe how her grandfather had also been a doctor, just like she was. This must have been where she got it from. She still didn't know the whereabouts of her birth mother, but she felt a real connection and an understanding of what she must have gone through as such a young girl.

She decided she'd tell James all about the contents of the letter when he came home from the hospital, and also resolved to go and visit the death camp where her father had been imprisoned – the notorious Auschwitz Birkenau.

James listened intently whilst Caitlin related the story of her mother and that of her Grandfather. He could see she was intent on visiting Auschwitz, as this was the only link she had to her real family. Although it was difficult for them both to be off work at the same time, they managed to arrange for a long weekend, Friday to Monday.

Krakow and Auschwitz

Caitlin wanted to spend the day in Krakow, since this was where her grandmother and grandfather had lived, but what was even more important to her was that they would visit Auschwitz, where her grandfather had been incarcerated and had lived a hell on earth existence.

Before she travelled to Poland to visit Krakow and the camp, she researched as much as she could about the history there. She learned that the first camp, known as Auschwitz One, had originally been barracks and then had been used as a prison for, so called political prisoners. The camp itself became fully operational in the spring of 1940, when Rudolph Höss was made camp commandant. Above the gates at the entrance gates there was a sign made in iron, containing the words, 'Arbeit Macht Frei' –'Work Makes You Free.'

The large majority of new arrivals deported to the camp were gassed, with the rest being starved, worked to death, or even killed in medical experiments. The renowned doctor, Joseph Mengele, known as the 'Angel of death,' carried out his diabolical experiments in Blocks 10 and 11 at Auschwitz One. The brick wall between these two buildings was known as the 'wall of death,' as many prisoners were murdered by firing squad when standing against this wall.

James and Caitlin had rented a small apartment in the old Jewish quarter of Krakow, close to where where the Jewish museum was situated. They took an early flight on Friday morning, so on Friday afternoon they began by paying a visit to the museum.

Caitlin purchased some relevant books from there and spoke to the curator. As she had no surname for her

Grandfather, it was impossible to search the archives for any information about him, but just by visiting Krakow, she felt she was paying tribute to her grandparents as this had been their home, and from where her grandfather had been taken and sent on that hellish journey in the cattle wagon to the terrible camp at Auschwitz.

Caitlin marvelled at the square in Krakow Old Town. She went inside the beautiful church and tried to imagine what it must have been like to be forced to leave all this behind.

They later ate in one of the many restaurants positioned along the streets leading out of the main square. Krakow certainly was a beautiful city.

Tomorrow was the day which Caitlin was both looking forward to, but at the same time, also dreading. She didn't really know what to expect from the visit.

After a one hour coach ride from Krakow bus station, they arrived at the gates of Auschwitz One and entered the camp. She was overcome with emotion as she viewed the cases containing crutches and artificial limbs, ones that contains shoes of all sizes and another which really touched her heart was full of baby clothes.

There were endless rows of photographs on the walls of those poor victims being forced to go there in a rush, after packing their most valuable items and family heirlooms, which had been on the orders they'd received. Whether they lived or died, they would never see these treasured items again.

They went round the site in complete silence. It seemed that most visitors spoke only in whispers out of respect for what had happened here all those years ago. Caitlin felt her heart racing and looked at James for support. She was so glad she had him there with her, to support her and hold her hand.

When they were ready, they took the free bus provided to take them to Auschwitz Two, better known as Auschwitz Birkenau.

As they entered by walking under the arched entrance to the camp, she became emotional. She couldn't help imagining what the people would have thought when arriving here all those years ago, arriving of course under very different circumstances.

"They must have been so scared, James," Caitlin said.

"Those poor bastards!" was all James could offer in return.

Caitlin recalled what her mother had said in her letter about the chimneys spewing out ash. No chimneys were here today, but there were still the watchtowers and the barbwire electric fences. How terrifying these must have been for the prisoners, with armed guards watching their every move and ready to pull the trigger at a split second! She learned that many prisoners had taken their own lives by attempting to climb, or simply throwing themselves at the electrified fences, rather than suffer any longer at the hands of the Nazi tormenters.

She'd been told this camp was the size of six thousand football pitches, but she still couldn't believe the massive expanse of it, it stretched for miles.

She visited the huts which were still standing, preserved so people could see the conditions these people lived in – if 'lived' was the correct use of the word!

People were living and sleeping three to a bunk, with the bunks three high, piled floor to ceiling. Caitlin saw the toilet and washing facilities, so few for so many prisoners and with no privacy whatsoever.

She went to the place where the hospital would have been, and where her Grandfather once worked. She stood in silence.

She'd learned how the prison doctors and orderlies all did their best at the time to save lives of sick prisoners, who were under constant threat of death from the SS doctors. They tried their best to keep them in care for as long as they possibly could. To save their lives, they would move them from hut to hut for further treatment. Caitlin believed this was the part her grandfather had played in saving many lives.

She laid a rose on the grass outside what would have been the hospital entrance and then went on to see the remains of the crematorium, where she visited the lakes of ashes. Standing at the lake, she really was all consumed with sadness. James held her arm to steady her.

"This is beyond belief" she said to James as he clung on to her.

"Man's inhumanity to fellow man," he replied.

Now very tired and weary, they returned to their apartment and packed their belongings in readiness for the early flight back to England the next morning.

Caitlin sat in stunned silence and said very little. James put his arm around her and they sat on the couch without speaking for much of the evening.

"Thank you," Caitlin finally whispered

"Thanks for what?" James questioned.

"For being here with me," she replied. "It was a terrible ordeal, but I had to do it. I have paid my respects to my family and now I feel a part of them."

She realised she may never find out who her birth mother really was, but she'd found her roots in the beautiful city of Krakow, a city which had been the home of her family.

She knew her grandfather had been a great man amd this was enough for her. She smiled at the thought of this.

She was now ready to marry the man whom she knew she loved, just as her mother had married the man she'd loved. Caitlin knew now that she'd been born from love, and that was all she needed to know.

As she'd now discovered her family history, she felt she was a real person at last and therefore felt she could marry James. She knew he was the right man for her. They worked so well together and understood some days at work were not easy, especially if they were unable to help a child, or if either or both of them needed time out to recharge their batteries. They were lucky to have such an understanding relationship, filled with love and mutual respect for each other.

Although not altogether romantic, they decided on a civil wedding with a couple of colleagues from the hospital to act as witnesses. They arranged it at the registry office together, having rescheduled their shifts early so they had just enough time to change into the clothes that they'd hurriedly bought for the occasion.

They were met at the door by the witnesses, and a very short time later they emerged as man and wife. Time for a swift jar at the local pub before returning to Caitlin's flat to get some much needed rest before their night shifts.

They loved each other and they were best friends. They also shared the commitment and love of their roles as paediatric doctors and needed nothing more than each other.

Their work meant they dealt with life and death in seemingly endless amounts. Sometimes they sat in silence, with Caitlin's head resting on James's shoulder, trying to make sense of what had happened that day at work.

Laura's Wedding

When he'd taken the call from his sister, Laura, announcing that she and Nikos were to be married, James was delighted for her. She informed him that she'd asked Yiannis, their mother's second husband to give her away, so she would like James to make the speech which John, their father would have made, had he been there. James was very happy and proud to be a part of his baby sister's celebrations.

He knew how Laura had come from an unhappy relationship, but had got her life back together again. She'd met Nikos and he'd taught her how to trust again and what love should really feel like.

Laura had been a tower of strength for Nikos after he was involved in a terrible accident. She'd helped him come to terms with the life altering injuries he'd endured, and now she was planning a new life as Nikos's wife. Big brother James was very proud for his sister. He could not have been any happier for her.

He spoke to Caitlin about the wedding and they both arranged the necessary cover at work so they could take time off together. Perhaps they could also make a holiday of it.

It was planned that they should stay with his mother, Jenny and her husband, Yiannis. They would also make time to spend with James's older sister, Suzie and her family. He was also very much looking forward to returning again to magical Kefalos.

Time passed quickly and it was soon time for them to fly to Kos. Suzie, Daniel and the girls had travelled a day earlier and were now staying with Laura in the home which had previously been their mother's home, built for Jenny and John, before he sadly passed away.

Jenny and her Greek husband, Yiannis, would be there at the airport to collect them. James hadn't really seen where they lived now, so he was looking forward to viewing it and staying there.

It was a long and winding road that led to the house. Secreted behind an outcrop of gorse trees, the house overlooked a beautiful little cove. James had learned that this cove was where his mother had met Yiannis, and had been special to both of them for various reasons. It was an idyllic setting, with fantastic views of the cove and the sea beyond it.

When they arrived at the home owned by Jenny and Yiannis, James thought the house was fabulous. He admired the exterior layout, as well as the tasteful interior.

Tonight, all the family would be reunited. Laura had arranged for them to eat at a favourite restaurant of theirs overlooking the Bay of Kamari. There was a lot in which to catch up, and as the Greeks do, they all talked at once, each wanting to relate their individual news and experiences. It was such a happy reunion of an extremely loving family.

After a lovely meal they sat chatting late into the night, with everyone feeling happy and loved. Two days from now would be the wedding, and James knew to expect it to be a very noisy affair. After all, most of the local villagers were likely to attend.

The setting was fabulous. The journey to the secluded beach by yacht was a great experience. His baby sister looked radiant when she arrived on the white yacht bedecked with flowers. He could see in her smile just how much she loved Nikos.

Yiannis led Laura along the carpet which stretched from the sea to the gazebo where several of the guests were seated, and where crowds of villagers were standing nearby, all delighted to see Nikos marry the beautiful English girl.

The ceremony was first in Greek, and then in English, ending with the traditional crossing and exchanging of headdresses tied with ribbons, thus binding the couple together.

After the ceremony everybody congregated in the large marquee which had been erected on the sand in the bay. Following a fantastic feast it was time for the speeches, so James took a large gulp from his glass of wine and nervously stood up.

His speech was short but so appropriate, stressing that he was delighted to talk about his baby sister and how much he admired the man she'd now married. He raised his glass to the man who should have been making this speech, knowing his father would have been overwhelmed at the beautiful lady his youngest daughter had grown up to become.

"Now, tradition has it that the father of the bride dances with his daughter," James said, "Today I will be taking the place of my dad, and it gives me great pleasure to fulfil the role he would have been so proud to take on."

The song, 'I loved you first' was played, and James skilfully manoeuvred his baby sister around the dance floor. When the song ended, he called Nikos to join his bride.

"She's all yours now, Nikos, please take care of her," he said to the groom.

"I will," Nikos smiled. "I promise I will always take care of your sister."

The evening was full of joy and happiness, with everyone joining in with the Greek dances and lots of cries of, "Opa."

James sat on the veranda of his mother's house a little later and held Caitlin's hand. "My dad would have been so proud today," he whispered. "He should have been here to see this." Caitlin squeezed his hand

"Just look at the sky," she told him, "Tonight it's full of stars. You told me your father said to look to the stars and he would always be there .I'm sure he's looking down on you now, and will be full of pride for the man you have become."

They continued to sit together in silence, just gazing at the beautiful night sky and at all the stars in attendance.

The time quickly came for James and Caitlin to return to England, back to life in the fast lane after the much more gentle life which it seemed Kefalos could offer them.

CHAPTER 3
A SURPRISE GIFT

James and Caitlin worked endlessly at the hospital now as paediatric specialists, and had little time for much else. They spent many nights sleeping at the hospital, since their shift patterns dictated it. Caitlin's flat was closest to the hospital, so if they did get away together they went there.

Hers was a little flat above a shop. She chose it for its closeness to medical school and the hospital, and at first it was sufficient for their needs. Now both established in the roles at the hospital they decided it was time to buy a home together. There were some nice properties on the outskirts of town with easy access to the hospital, and their combined salaries would easily allow them to buy a beautiful house together, which they did.

Now in their early forties they were happy with what they'd accomplished, and were content to dedicate themselves to their demanding work roles. They were also practical in their approach to their times apart because of shift patterns, spending quality time together when they were both off at the same time. Their lives revolved around the sick children within their care.

It was in the late spring when Caitlin began to feel unwell, being extremely tired and constantly uncomfortable. She tried vitamin supplements and asked to be relieved of some of her workload. She continued to be very tired and slept a lot, although she could not find a comfortable way to rest.

James had become increasingly concerned by her lack of energy, since she'd always been the one who could cope with the all nighters followed by the early shifts. In the end he insisted that she had some blood tested to see if she was anaemic.

"I think I might be going through the change of life, albeit a little early," Caitlin suggested.

"I think you need to see someone," James confirmed, to which she agreed.

The problem she had was that most of her friends were also her work colleagues, and because of this she felt a little embarrassed to speak to them. However, one close friend, Lucy, agreed to run a few tests, blood and urine for example. She arranged these tests for her friend, Caitlin.

"Can we meet? I have some important results for you." Lucy said when she rang Caitlin a few days after the tests had been completed.

Both were working that day, so they arranged to meet in the hospital canteen at lunchtime. Caitlin was feeling a little apprehensive when she later sat down with Lucy.

"Okay," Lucy began. "Your ECG heart and blood pressure are fine. Your blood is a little anaemic." She stopped to look at her friend before delivering the incredible news. "Your urine, well I checked this once and I checked it twice just to be certain, and I am one hundred percent sure. Caitlin, you're pregnant!"

Caitlin couldn't take this information in. James and she had never taken precautions once they'd married, but as she never became pregnant, they both accepted that this was how it was meant to be. Also, because their jobs were so demanding, but jobs they both loved so much, they never felt as though they'd missed out in anyway by not having a family.

"Are you okay, lovely?" Lucy asked. She smiled at her but received no answer. It was obvious to Lucy that her friend was very much in shock, so she continued with some advice. "Well then, the next step is we'd better tell the daddy, and then we'll speak to the antenatal department to make some appointments."

"Okay," Caitlin agreed, but obviously still in shock.

"Would you like me to ring James?" Lucy queried, as she didn't think at this moment in time, Caitlin was capable of doing this. Caitlin opened her mouth but no sound came. She nodded in agreement without speaking.

Lucy rang James and asked him," Can you meet Caitlin and me as soon as you can please?"

James came down from Theatre where he'd been operating, around twenty minutes later. Lucy could see concern already etched on his face, and when he looked at Caitlin his concern grew stronger. Her face was now ashen, and she was shaking.

"Darling whatever is wrong?" James pleaded. "Have you received the test results?" Caitlin nodded but said nothing. "Come on sweetheart, please, tell me what's wrong."

"I'm pregnant," Caitlin managed to whisper to James. "I'm, no, we're having a baby."

James's eyebrows shot up in utter amazement at this wonderful news. His heart was beating so fast, as like Caitlin, he'd written off any chances of ever having a child of his own.

"I think I'd like to go home now, James," Caitlin muttered still shaking. "It's all been a little bit of a shock."

"Of course, Darling," James said affectionately. "I'll finish up here and take you. Can you wait a few minutes?"

"It's okay James. I can take her home now," Lucy offered.

After thanking Lucy, James, ever the professional, shook all the thoughts of a possible child out of his mind whilst he struggled to save the life of another small infant.

Later as he drove home, he began to think about this news and how it would impact on their lifestyle and on Caitlin's ability to remain in such a demanding role at the hospital. She was still sitting peacefully, but still quite shocked when he reached home.

"How are you feeling now?" James asked.

"I'm not sure," she answered with honesty. "I just can't believe it after all this time. Lucy advised us to see a consultant."

"Then see a consultant is what we will do," James agreed with an air of confidence.

This was arranged and they attended an appointment a few days later, where scans were organised to determine just how many weeks pregnant Caitlin was. The consultant began to talk about what was always a difficult subject.

"Given your job and your knowledge, I know you're aware of the risks regarding pregnancy at your age. Unfortunately you are now classed as a geriatric mother, sorry. Once we establish how far along you are, I will be offering you an amniocentesis test to determine whether there are any genetic defects etcetera. I know you know all about this and I understand you know the risks with this test. The decision is up to you, but as a colleague and a friend, I would recommend, if you are able, to have this test carried out."

James smiled at Caitlin and squeezed her hand for support. He knew how shocked she had been by the discovery of her pregnancy, and now coming to terms with the possible risks there might be, was overwhelming.

When all the examinations and tests were completed, James and Caitlin were told that she was further along in her pregnancy than they'd first thought, so the invasive amniocentesis was not able to be done.

Although it had been confirmed that she could no longer take the test, Caitlin was unsure whether even if she could have, she would have risked it anyway.

Caitlin, although exhausted, carried the baby to full term. James and she were both apprehensive about how they would react to the baby, once it was born. Given her age and the possible problems for the baby, a caesarean section was recommended. The geriatric parents were both filled with anxiety.

James followed the trolley carrying Caitlin to the operating theatre. Wearing full scrubs, he stood beside the operating table and held Caitlin by the hand. He could feel the anxiety she felt flowing through her body but felt inadequate to allay her fears, as he was feeling much the same himself.

They both knew the consultant performing the operation, both agreeing he was the best at his job, but still the uncertainty frightened them.

Not long later, baby Grace was delivered. She was immediately rushed off to the waiting paediatric team. How many times had both James and Caitlin been involved in this procedure, giving all newborn babies the best possible chance they could, yet still they were anxious. Their daughter, Grace, was taken to neonatal intensive care.

James stood holding Caitlin's hand behind the surgery screen, whilst the consultant completed the rest of the operation. They would be invited down to the unit later, after all the necessary checks had been completed.

They hugged each other and cried, having been given a child they'd never expected, but both wondering whether it would survive, and if so, what quality of life might she have?

A wheelchair was bought for Caitlin and the new parents were later taken to the intensive care unit. This was their normal place of work, and their job would have been to tell the baby's anxious parents about what was going on and what to expect in the ICU, but this time, they were on the receiving end.

There before them in an incubator, was a chubby red faced little girl. She was breathing normally and waving her arms and legs around in the air like a wild thing. Everyone in the unit thought she was beautiful, especially to the new mum and dad.

They looked into the incubator and saw she was a Down's syndrome baby, but this didn't matter, because from the moment they laid eyes on their daughter they were overcome with an unconditional love for her. To some people her birth would be seen as a big mistake, something to hide under the carpet and not speak about, other people would sympathise with them because they hadn't had a normal baby.

Being in paediatrics all of their working lives, James and Caitlin knew the problems they may encounter, along with the stigma attached to a child that wasn't deemed perfect, but to them she was beautiful. She was their child, a child they'd never planned for and never expected to have.

Caitlin said she was a gift from God, and sent to complete their life. This was how they saw the baby. James said she was a precious star on loan to them, trying to be positive about the possible complications and setbacks and potential short life span that could affect their darling daughter.

Although she was a Downs syndrome child with the characteristic facial traits, she had Caitlin's dark hair colour, with James's deep brown eyes. Her hair grew longer and thick, and when tied up with ribbons and bows, she was such a pretty looking child.

When James's shifts allowed, they would put her to bed at night together. They felt blessed to have been given this one opportunity to be parents, and they loved it.

Usually, development goals for Downs's syndrome children were delayed, but Grace seemed to defy the odds. She sat up and crawled quite early, taking her first faltering steps before she was a year old, which was quite early.

Once a toddler she was into everything, giving both Mum and Dad something to smile about every day. Even on the days when James arrived home from a gruelling day at work, tired and exhausted, Grace filled him with renewed energy and purpose.

She was such a good baby, feeding and sleeping well. She was content and smiled a lot. As such she was the perfect baby, although because of the nature of their particular paediatric training they were well aware of the possible limitations regarding her intellectual growth.

They continued to rejoice in the role of parents, proud of every milestone regarding her development. Grace never ceased to amaze them with her achievements, even her speech, which, when she began to talk was incredibly easy to understand.

She continued to develop into a loving, accomplished little girl, full of life and full of fun. Everyone who came into contact with Grace fell in love with her immediately. She was very inquisitive, asking questions all the time just like any other little child. She had regular checkups at the hospital and James and Caitlin always monitored her constantly.

Family Holiday in Kefalos

At three years of age they took her for her first holiday abroad, and of course it was to Kos. Jenny had been eager to see her young grandchild in person, because Facetime and Skype were okay, but not the same as being able to hug her and spoil her.

At the airport, Caitlin pushed Grace in her buggy while James juggled the hand luggage and the special bag/backpack holding all the medication which Grace had to take everywhere, just in case of complications. At the hand luggage check, the security guard questioned James and asked about the contents of the backpack.

"It's mine," little Grace told the man. The guard's heart melted as she smiled at him. "Do you like the unicorns on my backpack?" she asked, and the security guard searching the buggy with Grace inside, was entranced by her smile.

When they boarded the aircraft, Grace's big eyes opened even wider. She was amazed to see how many seats there were. She understood why she had to be strapped in and seemed quite at ease with the situation. When the aircraft began to take off she looked a little apprehensive and held tight to Mum's hand.

The flight itself was quite uneventful, and when they landed with a bump on the runway, Grace couldn't contain her excitement and clapped her hands frantically as they landed on the island.

James carried her through passport control and Grace made the official smile by telling him, "That's me in the picture," as he scrutinised her passport.

Once the buggy came through on the baggage conveyor, Grace was placed in it and strapped in. It was far too busy a place for her to wander off. Once they had their luggage, they exited through the sliding doors and spotted Laura frantically waving to them.

Grace was really excited, as she would get to meet her cousins for the first time. Laura had told them all about Grace, how she was a 'special little girl' and they were looking forward to meeting her, along with Uncle James and Auntie Caitlin.

Laura had fitted a car seat for Grace in the four by four and all could see that she was really enjoying this new experience. With everything now loaded, they set off from the airport en-route to Kefalos.

There had been no hesitation when Dimitris and Toula met Grace for the first time. They sat on the floor with her and played with their toys. They later took her to the pool, complete with armbands, where watched over by parents and family they played happily together. Although they'd been very protective of Grace for so long they could see how much the family were looking after her, and so James and Caitlin were able to relax a little more.

At the end of this fun filled day in Kefalos, little Grace was exhausted. .James and Caitlin put her down in the special toddler bed which Laura had prepared. With her arms wrapped around her favourite teddy, she slept soundly through the night, until the morning sun peeked through the curtains.

Today, the first full day of their visit, they would introduce Grace to the beach. She loved her sandpit at home, but James wondered how she would react to the expanse of sand and the moving water, with the waves crashing on the beach. They had chosen Cavos Beach, the one near the harbour, since the water here was calm and shallow.

James carried Grace down the steps to the beach, and wide eyed, the youngster looked at the beach and the sea for the very first time.

"Look Daddy, big bath" was her response to the expanse of water before her. Everybody laughed when hearing her say this.

Dimitris and Toula took her by the hand and walked to the water's edge, where the sea gently caressed her tiny toes. She backed away a little then stepped back into the water.

"Splash," she cried, as she bent down and put her fingers in the sea, throwing water over her cousins.

"Splash" they cried back to her, splashing her knees. Grace liked this game and laughed and clapped her hands.

James, Caitlin and Laura watched, enjoying the interaction between their children. They made sandcastles and sand pies and everyone enjoyed their experience.

"Boat," Grace shouted, as a black yacht entered the Harbour area. It was Laura's husband, Nikos.

"Boat," she shouted again.

"Do you want to go on the boat, Grace?" James asked.

"Yes, boat," Grace replied.

They cleared up the beach things and walked down to the harbour together, where Nikos had brought the dinghy from the yacht. He first collected Laura and their two children and took them to the yacht, and then returned for James, Caitlin and Grace.

Little Grace put her hands over her ears as the outboard motor was started. She looked a little anxious and held on tightly to James as they made their way to the waiting yacht. When reaching it, they passed Grace up to the waiting arms of Laura and then clambered aboard themselves. The sea was very calm today, and because of this there was very little movement on the yacht.

Nikos had brought fresh spanakopita, spinach pies and Tiropita, cheese pies from the bakers in the village, along with freshly baked baklava as a sweet.

As she ate the food, Grace pondered on the new taste of spinach, but didn't seem too impressed. She did however love the cheese pies and the sweet tasting Baclava.

"Shall we try a little sail now?" Nikos suggested, and everyone was in agreement.

Nikos expertly piloted the boat from the harbour and they sailed across the bay, passing close to the island of Kastri with its tiny Church of Saint Stephanos perched on the rocks. James remembered it well, as it was where his mother had chosen to marry Yiannis, and where he'd witnessed the love between them.

They rounded the rocky headland and came to Camel Beach, a shale beach with dark sand, and then on past the famous Paradise Beach and Bubble Beach, with its Jacuzzi type bubbles which came from the volcanic island of Nissyros opposite.

They went round the headland, where Club Robinson had their hotel, and it was here where Nikos turned the yacht about and they cruised back to the Bay of Kamari.

Whilst the parents sat in 'Bravo,' the children played on the beach below, under the watchful eye of James and Caitlin.

James began to think what a wonderful life Grace could have living here with her cousins on this beautiful island, away from the hustle and bustle of city life in England. He wondered if he should suggest that Caitlin came here for the summer with Grace, but then he thought how much he would miss his little girl, as well as, of course, his wife.

If only there was an opportunity here for him to work here, but that wasn't going to happen, so they were to enjoy the time they had here with his sister, Laura and her family.

Time passed so quickly and soon it was time to return home to England. Back to work for James, and back to caring for Grace at home for Caitlin.

Although she had friends in the hospital in England she began to realise how important family was, and how much she'd enjoyed being with Laura and her family. She'd also enjoyed her time on the island with James's mother, Jenny and Yiannis. Caitlin had lost her parents at a young age and was for a long time an only child, so she had not experienced much family life and now realised what both she and Grace were missing in their lives.

The last evening before the departure to England, Laura, Nikos, James and Caitlin chatted about life in Kefalos, about the different lifestyles they had. James felt a pang of guilt that he was unable to give his wife and daughter the lifestyle which Laura and her family had, and expressed this in his chat with them.

Goodbyes were said, tears were shed, and promises were made to return to Kefalos for another holiday, "Very soon." Laura and Nikos waved as they went through the doors of the departure lounge and the doors slid closed behind them. Nikos could see the sadness in Laura's eyes and put his arm around her shoulders.

"What are you thinking?" he asked. "Tell me what you are thinking."

"I just wish my brother and his family could come and live here. It would be wonderful for me, and also for Grace," Laura said.

Nikos squeezed her hand. "If it's in the stars, then it will happen," he told her.

She wanted so much to believe this. Her father had always told her to look to the stars, and Nikos had told her when the stars align they would get to see their wishes come true.

Now, yet again, it was the stars that had to be relied on.

CHAPTER 4
AN AMAZING OFFER

Life went on in sunny Kefalos. Dimitris attended the local school and Toula the Infant School. Nikos continued with his role as director of the business, whilst Laura was busy being the perfect Greek wife and mum.

Nikos watched her and could see that although she was happy there was something missing. He thought long and hard how he could fill the gap and spent time with his lawyer and accountant discussing possibilities. When a viable plan was finally created, Nikos spoke to Laura.

"Do you think James would move here if he had the right job opportunity?" he questioned his wife. "He did say he would love to live here when we chatted when they were here on holiday."

Laura screwed her eyes up inquisitively, so Nikos continued to question her by asking, "Do you think Caitlin would like to move here with Grace?"

"Okay," Laura replied, curiously looking him in the eye. "What have you been planning?"

"I need to talk to James before I say anything more," he admitted, winking and smiling in her direction.

It was a long and possibly life changing telephone conversation between Nikos and James. Nikos had worked out how he would ask his brother in law in a way so as to not appear condescending or laud his own financial situation over him. After pleasantries were exchanged on the phone, Nikos began in earnest, telling James the reason for the call.

"I want to build a paediatric centre here on the island as a thank you for all the help both Laura and I received from the medical staff on the island when we needed it," Nikos began.

"Whilst I can possibly find the clerical and nursing staff from here, I need an experienced paediatrician in situ. The salary would be equivalent to that of the NHS in England, and I would like to offer you the position first."

James couldn't believe what he was hearing. He'd never stopped searching for an opportunity to take his wife and daughter to Kos. Of course there would be lots of things to discuss and plans to be made, but wow, what a wonderful opportunity he'd been given. Nikos told James to chat with Caitlin about it and let him know if they were interested so he could get the ball rolling.

James put the phone down and felt overwhelmed by what had just transpired. It was what he had hoped and prayed for, for such a long time, and here it was, now being offered to him.

James had always liked Nikos and felt no animosity towards him for his financial situation. He saw what a kind man he was and how generous he'd been to the community of Kefalos, but most of all, James could see how much he loved Laura. Nikos was proud to be from Kefalos, and he wanted to give it everything it truly needed.

James went through to the lounge, where Caitlin was sitting on the floor playing with Grace. She looked up at him and could see excitement in his eyes as he smiled at her.

"I've just had a call from Nikos," he told her

"Is everything okay?" Caitlin questioned with concern in her voice.

"Everything's fine," he smiled. "In fact it's more than fine and I have a big question to ask you. How would you like to move to Kefalos?" he smiled again. Her reply was extremely prompt.

"Ha ha, you already know my answer to that question," she said, with a broad smile in return.

James got the idea that his wife thought he was joking, so said, "Seriously, would you consider selling up and moving out to Kefalos?" he said. He searched her face again for a reaction to his question.

"But we can't. There are no jobs for you there," she said sadly, realising it was a serious question

"But if there were, how would you feel about it?" he asked again, pushing her for an answer.

"I think it would be the most wonderful thing for Grace and you, and my whole purpose in life, apart from loving you, is to give Grace the best things possible in her life, and I believe her life would be enriched by living in a place like Kefalos," she said, now grinning like a Cheshire cat.

"That, my darling is the answer I needed," he confirmed.

He went on to tell Caitlin about Nikos's offer, and what his involvement would be in the planning of the centre.

"But where would we live?" Caitlin questioned.

"Nikos has proposed to build us a house," James revealed.

Caitlin listened to her husband intently. This was a dream come true for them. Could it really be happening? Was it actually in the stars for them to live on the beautiful Greek island of Kos, living a completely different life to the one they had now? She truly hoped so much that it was.

James telephoned Nikos with their decision. Both Nikos and Laura were thrilled when they heard what James and Caitlin had decided, and couldn't wait to get things going.

Now that they'd decided to move to Kefalos and take up Nikos's wonderful offer, the next thing to look at was a home for the three of them. Nikos asked James to tell him exactly what he wanted, what special facilities they may need for Grace, and exactly where they would like to live. He told them they had a 'blank canvas' and everything was entirely up to them.

James and Caitlin couldn't believe it. They would have had funds to buy somewhere from the sale of their home in

England, but what Nikos was offering was way beyond their budget or wildest dreams.

They considered all the things which would be vital, certainly a wet room for Grace adjoining her bedroom, along with a playroom for her. They thought it would be better all round if the house was completely built on one level. Although it seemed an absolute dream to them, Nikos suggested a pool incorporating safety issues for Grace, so that she could continue with her hydrotherapy at home.

The garden would need to be child friendly and with security, so Grace wouldn't wander off and get into trouble. Everything seemed to revolve around ensuring everything was suited for Grace. The way their life had been before Grace, they'd had little time at home. Although they had a beautiful house, they'd never really made it a real home. It had not been high on their priorities until Grace was born.

Nikos took all the suggestions to his architect and he drew up plans for them. With technology, James and Caitlin were able to see what storage space was included, furniture and kitchens planned, outside and inside areas carefully designed to take in the best views and make best use of the space available. It was their dream house, a house built for a family, their family, with every last requirement taken care of, with more besides.

Nikos owned a lot of land close to his own Villa in the village of Kefalos. He suggested a plot adjacent to his home. This plot offered fantastic views and they were in close contact with him and Laura, plus the children would be able to see each other often.

Once everything had been finalised, work began on the property. James and Caitlin had to begin considering the children's centre. Nikos told James that money was no object.

He wanted to repay the community for the life they'd given him here in his beloved Kefalos.

James and Caitlin's house in England sold quickly, as it was in a good area and close to the hospital, so it was sold to a fellow worker.

They had furnished it to minimal standards, as they'd only seemed to sleep there between shifts. It was only since Grace was born that they'd accumulated more items.

James knew that the house in Kefalos would be fully furnished, with everything they needed for themselves and for Grace, so only precious items and Grace's favourite toys would be travelling out to Kos with them.

Because of the milder Greek climate, winter woollies would not be needed in such abundance as in the UK, and the local charity shops were delighted to receive clothes and small items, whilst the larger national charities which had warehouses were keen to accept items of furniture and children's items. Tomorrow they would take taxis to the airport, as both their cars had also been sold.

James awoke from his slumber. He'd visited his past and it had shown him why he was making this gigantic move. In his mind, he'd promised that he would give his family the life his sister Laura had in Kefalos, and the life his mother had chosen before that. He would give all he had to this wonderful offer from his brother in law. He finished the final packing and was now ready for tomorrow.

The next morning, they stood in the house and looked at the empty rooms. The luggage was at the airport ready for transportation, they'd said their goodbyes to family and friends, and now they were on their way to their new lives in Kos. It was the end of an era.

Nikos was there to collect them at the airport. With all the cases easily placed in the boot of the large four by four, they began the short trip from the airport to Kefalos, a road they now knew well. Grace was strapped securely into the car seat next to Caitlin, whilst James sat in the front alongside Nikos.

No need for the tourist guide spiel today as James could name the various beaches along the route in his sleep. He still loved to watch through the window though, guessing which one was next. Caitlin had butterflies in her stomach. She hoped it wouldn't be too stressful for Grace dealing with a new life in unfamiliar surroundings.

"Laura is at the house waiting for us. She's done some shopping for you and made up the beds I hope you will like everything we've done," said Nikos.

"I'm sure we will," James smiled. "And thank you very much."

"Don't mention it," Nikos replied.

The short journey from the airport was over quickly. The car now climbed up the hill to the village of Kefalos and once through, they drove to the villa which was to be their home. With their first glimpse of the building they saw there was a walled garden surrounding the house.

Caitlin gasped as they approached. It was even more beautiful than in the video and photographs they'd seen. The large electrical gate swung open and allowed them to enter the garden and drive up the gravel path to the front door. Grace had been quiet for most of the car ride, but she clapped her hands frantically as she was lifted from her car seat.

Laura opened the door and rushed out. For a moment, Grace hid behind her mother but then she sensed it was okay, so peeped out. Laura held out her arms and Grace recognised her and ran to her.

"Welcome to your new home," Laura said, smiling from ear to ear. She was so excited to find out whether her big brother was pleased with all her hard work, setting up the home for him and his family.

James hugged his baby sister. He was so appreciative of what she'd achieved, ensuring everything went smoothly and nothing was missed. They walked round the house in awe of the size of it and all the beautiful furnishings.

Grace, her big eyes wide open with excitement, was running around opening doors and shouting with glee at everything she saw. When she found a room containing toys and a special bed, she knew this was the bedroom for her. It wasn't long before she crawled onto the bed and fell asleep, exhausted by all the travel and excitement of the day.

Laura had prepared a meal and left it all in the amazing, very large American style fridge, situated inside the equally large kitchen. Caitlin was completely lost for words when she saw the kitchen with its ultra modern appliances, beautiful family size breakfast bar and fully equipped utility room leading from it.

Nikos showed James all the security systems and the pool mechanics, and then he and Laura left them alone to settle in and get comfortable. When they were alone, Caitlin looked at James with a look of contentment.

"It's just wonderful. We are so lucky, James," Caitlin sighed.

"Well from tomorrow, we begin working to pay for it," he laughed.

Tomorrow they would check the progress of the centre so far. The plans had been seen and poured over on numerous occasions, and now it was James's job to design and fill it with all the equipment needed and to meet the staff employed by Nikos, and to familiarise himself with everything. He took a deep breath as he thought about the task before him, hoping he could rise to the occasion.

"I hope I'm worthy of the trust Nikos has put in me," he said to Caitlin.

"Of course you are," she reassured hm. "And I'll be here at your side every step of the way."

"Thank you, Darling," James beamed.

"We've been through so much together," Caitlin continued. "I know we can, and will make a success of our new life here."

"Thank you, "James said again, and this time he received a kiss on the cheek.

"Come on, let's check out our room," Caitlin suggested. "Grace seems happy with hers. She's already fast asleep."

"Check out our bedroom?" James said. He winked at her and taking her by the hand, led her to their 'special room.'

He thanked his lucky stars that Caitlin had come into his life all those years ago. She'd been at his side through thick and thin. There is no way he could have wished for a more loving and supportive wife.

They slept soundly after their lovemaking, entwined in each other's arms and waking later to see the sun shining behind the blinds.

A little voice called out to them, followed by Grace walking into the room and smiling at them. She held tight to her favourite teddy as she was a little apprehensive about where she was, but having her mum and dad there was enough for her to feel safe. She jumped on the bed, snuggled up with them and smiled.

"Hey, I have to go to work," James announced and then tickled Grace until she laughed and laughed. Mum and Dad never tired of seeing her happy face.

Their first breakfast was eaten at the breakfast bar. Laura had shopped for everything they could ever think of, which was good, as they were all hungry after their long journey the day before.

After breakfast they readied themselves for the short journey to the building site where the centre was under construction. Nikos was there to meet them and show them the progress which had been made. James could see that the attention to detail regarding the position and the panorama from up here on the hill above the village was incredible. Large windows offered views across both sides of the island.

The centre was situated on a large plot with an extensive garden area, which James knew would include a safe play area for children staying at the centre. They carefully ventured inside the building, avoiding ladders, building materials and construction tools. No inside walls had been built yet, giving James the opportunity to choose exactly where he would like various rooms for offices, reception areas, theatres, therapy rooms and any others required.

At this moment it seemed so big and empty, but he knew that soon the rooms would be filled with the equipment he'd chosen, and would be decorated so that every room was child centred and child friendly. He was feeling a little overwhelmed at having been given such an opportunity.

He knew the sooner he began organising things, the sooner the centre would be up and running and helping the children of Kos. James had done a lot of research and had written list after list. He'd done costing of equipment, estimates of maintenance costs and staffing requirements.

He always included Caitlin in his decision making, and constantly asked for her advice and approval. They worked so well together as a team, and when the centre opened they would be working side by side, as always.

Months later the centre was fully furnished and equipped, staff had been brought in for training, and they were almost ready for the opening ceremony, which would take place in a few weeks from now.

James stood and surveyed the dream centre he'd created and looked across at Nikos by his side. It was Nikos who'd funded everything amd without him, James knew that none of this would have been possible, and for this, he was eternally grateful.

"We have created something very special here," James said, hugging his Greek brother in law, "and it's all thanks to you."

"I couldn't have done any of this without you," Nikos said in reply, smiling.

"Thank you Nikos," James said, almost in a whisper. He was beginning to get emotional and Nikos, noticing this, slapped him n the back.

"Well, James," Nikos shouted. "Are you ready to live the dream?" James nodded in agreement.

"Nikos, I am more than ready," he replied.

CHAPTER 5
THE GRAND OPENING

It was the day of the grand opening of the paediatric centre. The local mayor had been asked to cut the ribbon across the entrance of the doors and open the premises officially. All the appointed staff waited outside to greet the mayor, with Nikos and Laura being there to hand over the centre to the community.

Many of the villagers had gathered to watch the opening as a tribute to Nikos for his generosity, whilst others had come just to get a look at the new English manager of the centre. They'd heard he was highly qualified and a dedicated practitioner with years of experience attending to children's medical and surgical needs. Only time would tell how the English couple would be fully accepted. Although they'd always been made to feel welcome as visitors to Kefalos, James and Caitlin would need to gain their trust.

Everyone was excited to see the inside of the new centre, and they were not disappointed. Thanks to Nikos and James, it had been expertly planned and contained all the latest equipment. There were operating theatres, therapy rooms and family rooms, built so parents could remain with their children. There were play rooms for recovery, along with children safe areas for kids with special needs. Everything was bright and the walls were covered in colourful murals, making it a friendly place for the youngsters.

Happy smiley uniformed staff showed people around, explaining what each room would be used for and what purpose the equipment had.

Drinks and snacks were available outside the centre, so people could stand and chat with, and get to meet the members of the team who'd be running, and working at the centre.

It had been a fantastic achievement in building such a complex building, but tomorrow the real work would begin. Tomorrow the work would begin to establish the centres reputation as the place to take care of any children's needs, medically, physically, mentally, and emotionally.

Nikos smiled as he watched James and Caitlin chatting to the locals as best they could, with the enormous language barrier. They were speaking with locals, mums carrying babies in arms and some with toddlers holding fast to their hands. Some had come from neighbouring villages, all interested in this new project.

When the last visitor had finally left, Nikos, Laura, James and Caitlin stood together at the front of the building. There were magnificent views from here and there was peace and serenity about the surrounding gardens and play areas. Nikos was pleased with the response of his fellow residents to this venture. He was sure that, managed by James and his team, it would prove to be a great success.

The first to bring their children to the centre were families that Nikos knew and felt comfortable with what he'd created. Slowly, by word of mouth, more people brought their children to the centre.

All the members of staff were really happy to answer questions, quell concerns of any anxious parents, and give advice on vaccination assessment procedures.

In the early days it was quieter than James and Nikos had expected, with James's expertise not really being stretched. One day, whilst dealing with a minor injury a commotion could be heard in reception, with considerable amounts of shouting and wailing going on. The emergency siren was heard.

"Come quickly!" shouted the receptionist.

Everyone ran to the reception area where a man was carrying the lifeless body of a small child. The man shouted something in Greek to James, while h man's wife kept screaming and wailing. The man didn't want to relinquish his hold on the child and James had to prise him from his arms.

James rushed through the swing doors carrying the child, leaving the parents not knowing what to do. One of the nurses spoke to them in Greek and reassured them that James was a great doctor and would do everything he could for their child.

The nurse asked the parents questions about what had happened, and how their child had come to be in this state.

Meanwhile, James and his team had laid the child on the table in the resuscitation room. The child wasn't breathing and he was beginning to turn blue around the mouth. Machines were attached to take readings, which showed his heartbeat was very faint. Maybe it was too late for this child, but James was not about to give up!

Whatever had caused the infant to collapse may have happened over a period of time. James searched to discover a cause, whilst others of the team administered oxygen. They looked for blocked airways, in case he'd swallowed something and it was obstructing his windpipe.

The machine now showed his heartbeat was becoming more and more faint, so the team carried on with resuscitation techniques but suddenly then the heart stopped! Lights flashed and monitors beeped, letting them all know that life was leaving this little one's body. It was time for James to make a radical decision.

Instructing his team as to what he was about to do, he began to operate on the child. He was determined that he would not fail this little one on the operating table. He opened up the chest cavity and began to massage the child's heart with his hands, but as the crew looked on, the monitors still showed no output from the heart.

Vital seconds passed as he continued to massage the tiny heart, but then a slight bleep-bleep sound was heard from the monitor and a few seconds later it was heard again.

"Come on, fight," James whispered. "You can do this, little one."

Slowly and miraculously the heart began to beat normally and the machines could now take over. There was still a long way to go, but now the little heart was causing the blood to circulate in his once blue body, which was now beginning to return to pink. James pulled the breast bone together and closed the gaping hole in the chest.

Over the next few hours the child would be monitored constantly, and once stabilised they'd begin trying to discover what had caused this cardiac arrest in such a young child.

It was time to speak to the parents who'd been waiting patiently, not knowing if their child had survived or not. As James walked into the waiting room both parents stood up and looked at him with tearful eyes and expressions of fear, beseeching the doctor to give them some good news.

"Please sit down," James directed them. "Your little boy is still in a very critical condition," he said, with a nurse translating what he was saying. "Your son had stopped breathing and his heart stopped beating," James went on to tell them.

"My God," the mother stressed, crossing herself.

"I had to perform an unusual operation," James revealed. "I had to open his chest and massage his heart to start it beating again."

"But will he be okay," the father pleaded and then hung his head in sorrow.

"He's breathing now with the help of machines, but his heart is beating normally at the moment," James instructed. "It's too early to make any judgement on his condition. We will keep him sedated and we'll watch him and deal with any changes over the next day or two. He seems to be a strong child and definitely a fighter, so let's pray to God that he can get over this critical stage," James offered.

"Can we see him?" both parents asked simultaneously.

"Not at the moment," James told the parents.

He went on to explain that there were too many machines attached to his little body for them to enter the room safely. He told them they could briefly look at their son through the window, but as the team had to work on him constantly, they would only be able to look for a minute or two. They agreed to this and so the nurse took them to see their child.

James suddenly felt exhausted. He decided to go to the restroom, but to stay alert in case there were any changes to the boy's condition.

With each day, little Costas became more mobile and animated. He didn't like to have his dressings changed and in true Greek fashion, yelled and screamed as if he was being tortured!

His recovery continued and soon it was time for the child to go home. James was there to say goodbye and release him to the care of his parents.

It was characteristic of the centre to take the patient to the front door of the clinic, where in a sense their responsibility ended at the main sliding doors. As the main sliding doors opened, a massive cheer went up from the outside. It seemed like all the residents of the village were standing outside and clapping .It was a fantastic show of appreciation for the man who had saved a local village boy, a boy who it was said had died and been brought back to life by the man from England.

"I was just doing my job," James told the crowd, feeling overwhelmed. "I was just doing what I was trained to do," he said. However, no one agreed with him. He had gone far beyond this and was now, in the eyes of the people, a hero and superstar.

From that day on, James was accepted by the village, and Kefalos was now his and Caitlin's home.

"Let's go and relax now," James said to his Greek brother in law. Nikos put his hand on James's shoulder and they walked together out of the centre.

They called into Corner Café and James was surprised when people sitting there came across to shake hands with him. It seemed he'd become an overnight celebrity, and for the next few weeks, wherever he went he was greeted and admired, and people showed him an enormous amount of gratitude for what he had done.

Living the Dream

Whenever possible, James, Caitlin and daughter, spent time together as a family. They visited the beach and took Grace to see the Peacocks at Plaka. They went with Laura, Nikos and their children and they all swam in the sea. They also celebrated all the Greek festivals and never a day went by when James wasn't thankful for Nikos giving him the opportunity to move here to Kos, this beautiful island.

Grace was staying with Aunty Laura and Uncle Nikos today, and was happy to be with her cousins, Dimitris and Toula.

It was a balmy evening, so James and Caitlin drove to Kochylari Beach. It was deserted, apart from a few Seagulls scavenging amongst the seaweed along the shore. The two walked hand in hand in silence, not speaking, as it would have broken the beautiful tranquillity of the moment. The only sound heard was the lapping of the waves as they gently caressed the shore. James stopped and turned Caitlin around to face him.

"We never really had a proper wedding, did we?" he began. "Our lives were so embroiled in our work that we never really thought about each other. We've had intimate moments in our life, but romance has never played a big part.

Having Grace changed our lives completely and made us realise the more important things. She changed our lives and she changed us.

More and more, I have come to know real love and contentment. I love my work but I so love my family, and they are now what gives me real pleasure and satisfaction. I don't think I've ever really made one romantic gesture in all my life, but here I am, now almost overcome by emotion in this beautiful setting.

I look at you and see a beautiful woman, my soul mate, my wife, the mother of my daughter and my rock. I can't really kneel on this sand, but Caitlin, will you marry me again, but properly this time?"

Caitlin was stunned! James was a lovely, caring man, who she had loved deeply for many years, but he'd always held his feelings in check.

Of course she knew he loved her, a little touch from his hand or a flick of her hair, a peck on the cheek, or a soft pat on her bottom as she passed him. He'd never really testified his love for her, and these words were truly from the heart. How could she say no to him, not that she wanted to. His big eyes scanned her beautiful face and searched for a reaction.

"My darling James, of course I'll marry you here," she replied, lifting her hands and touching his cheek.

As the light of the day left them, and the shadows deepened, here on the deserted beach he lay her down in the soft sand and made love to her. After all the years they'd been together, this intimate moment took their relationship to a whole new level. This was real love.

"So how do we plan this wedding?" James asked later.

"Ask your mother and Laura," Caitlin suggested. "They've both married on Kos, so know what has to be done."

"That's a great idea," James announced.

I would like to get married on the little island, if that's okay with you?" Caitlin queried. "It's always seemed to me to be such a magical place." James looked at Caitlin and smiled.

"This is going to sound crazy," he began. "But just looking at you here in front of me now makes me feel like I'm falling in love with you all over again. I know I have loved you since I first set eyes on you, but now I'm falling in love with the real you."

Caitlin smiled. She knew exactly what he meant, because she also felt exactly the same way. Here in this wonderful place they had found each other as individual people, not as classmates or work colleagues, not as father and mother, but as themselves, two people in love.

They told Laura first about how they intended to renew their vows and wanted to do it in the little church on the island of Kastri, as Jenny had done all those years ago.

Laura and Nikos were delighted for them. In their minds it cemented their transition to being real residents of Kefalos, and Laura was only too happy to help them organise the event.

She suggested they send an open invitation to the village of Kefalos after the blessing and their reception would be arranged as a barbecue on the beach, so all the local people could come and go at will. It sounded perfect to the happy couple.

When they heard of the details, James's mother, Jenny and her husband, Yiannis, were delighted to hear of their plans. It brought back such happy memories of their own wedding on the little island. Jenny remembered the drive in the horse and cart which had taken them down to the harbour, the boat ride to the island, and friends and family who'd come to Kefalos to join them in the ceremony. It had been a wonderful occasion, and she hoped now that her son would also have happy memories to treasure in the future.

As with Laura's wedding, the white yacht taking Caitlin and Yiannis to the island had been decked with flowers, whilst another boat had already taken the rest of the family and guests to the island.

James stood with Nikos, impatiently awaiting Caitlin's arrival. Nikos was to act as best man for James, whilst Laura was chief bridesmaid for Caitlin. Grace, as a bridesmaid, was absolutely delighted by all the extra attention she was receiving.

Caitlin had chosen to wear an off the shoulder, full length dress of ecru coloured lace, matched with a tiny hat with a veil. She remembered the hurriedly bought store brand dress she'd worn for the actual wedding ceremony, all those years ago in the tiny registry office.

James and Caitlin stood in front of the little church on the island of Kastri to renew their vows to each other, surrounded by their family. This time it wasn't to be the hurried ceremony they'd experienced in the registry office, with just two guests as witnesses. That marriage ceremony had seemed the right thing to do at the time given their busy schedules, but this time it was a lovely family occasion, with the three generations of the family all here together.

They looked straight into each other's eyes as they repeated the vows they'd written, expressing their feelings of the love and devotion they felt for each other. It was an emotional and uplifting experience for them all. They now felt truly blessed with what life had handed them.

How proud Jenny was of her entire family. She couldn't help but think that John would have been extremely proud to see his son, now such an accomplished surgeon, a loving and caring man and a good husband, but above all, a wonderful father to his much loved special daughter.

CHAPTER 6
SURVIVING THE ELEMENTS

Summer had arrived again and the vicious heat had returned. There had been no rain for months on the island and the land around Kefalos was parched and literally tinder dry.

One early morning, when James went into the garden he smelled a certain something in the air which was not the usual fragrant smell from the land. With horror, he realised it was the smell of burning vegetation.

The high walls surrounding the villa prevented him from seeing much of the surrounding land, so he rushed down to the entrance gate. He looked across to where Nikos and Laura's villa stood, but could see nothing there. The smell was growing stronger and the air was getting hazy.

He looked up at the centre and there on the hillside he could see smouldering grass, but when the wind blew it changed to bright red flames reaching up the hillside and heading towards the centre. Frantically he ran back to the house to phone the fire brigade.

"Caitlin," he shouted to his wife when he ran inside the door and saw her standing there. "Grab hold of Grace and get ready to move," he demanded.

The fear he felt when he thought they might lose their beloved home produced all the adrenaline needed to spur him along. He rang Nikos and warned him, and Laura got some things together in case the fire eventually reached them.

Nikos reacted quickly and turned on all the sprinklers in the garden, and using the hosepipe he drenched all the trees and shrubs, forming a natural protective barrier around the villa.

James made his way to the centre and saw that the fire was rapidly burning up the valley and heading towards it. He knew that at this moment there were no children inside the building, but all the precious equipment was at risk. Thousands and thousands of euros had been spent on the centre and it must be protected.

Eventually fire engines arrived from stations all over the island and began to attempt to hold the spread. Everywhere was so dry it was easy for the flames to take hold. When the wind blew, the flames spread it in all directions like long fingers.

James stayed close to the centre, as this was the place most threatened if the fire couldn't be controlled.

Whilst the firemen worked tirelessly, villagers came up to the centre to help James, and on his instructions they hosed down the exterior walls of the centre.

A helicopter was mobilised and it scooped water from the sea in a large bucket located underneath the chassis. Several times it flew over, releasing the captured water where the fire was at its worst, before returning to the sea to fill up and repeat the process all over again.

Suddenly a gust of wind shot the flames within metres of the main gates of the centre and James feared the worst. He was scared that this wonderful centre, which had done so much for the local community, could very well be lost.

The helicopter was seen again hovering above the top of the smouldering valley, and water again gushed from the bucket and cascaded down from it quelling the flames. Below, on the ground the fireman continued to hose and beat the vegetation. Whatever happened next was totally in the lap of the gods, or indeed in the hands of Mother Nature.

James hadn't prayed for years, but he began to now. He was comforted in the fact that he knew that at the present time, his and Nikos's homes were both safe.

Maybe it was his prayers being answered because suddenly the wind changed direction. Perhaps it was one of the quirks of the winds on the island, but it happened anyway.

With all the help they'd had, they managed to stem the flow of the fire for the time being. At this present time, the centre had been saved.

"It will be several hours before the fire brigade will declare it as under control," one of the fire officers informed James.

Several little fires were still smouldering and they would have to ensure that all these had been extinguished before they left, since the change of wind could start it all up again.

Caitlin and Grace had been waiting down the hillside, terrified that something had happened to James, as he had been gone so long.

James stood there, his eyes streaming from the acrid smoke, his throat feeling like he'd swallowed sandpaper, but he believed that he'd just witnessed a miracle. The centre itself had been left totally undamaged, although the fire had raged all around the centre and the perimeter garden had been affected. The fire had damaged all the plants and the play areas.

James stayed a little longer, but then went home to his family. Arriving home, he hugged both Caitlin and Grace as if their lives depended on it. He was so thankful that this disaster had ended and been averted, and a few days later, the villagers rallied together to restore the beautiful gardens and the centre's play areas.

James realised from that day just how precious life was and how fragile it could be. They could have lost everything that day, even their lives. He also had it re-affirmed just how wonderful the local Greek residents really were.

A couple of weeks after the great fire of Kos, James was back in the theatre and about to carry out a very delicate operation, as ever, with Caitlin standing by his side. Since the two had renewed their marriage vows on the beautiful island in the bay, their relationship had changed very much to being even more in love.

Although masks covered their faces, when James smiled across at Caitlin she knew he was smiling by his eyes, they said it all. She nodded back to him.

Everything was prepared for the operation when all the instruments arranged on the medical table suddenly began to shake and rattle. The framed certificates on the walls began to swing from side to side, and the floor beneath their feet started to vibrate, moving up and down and from side to side.

"Earthquake!" one of the theatre nurses shouted. Although there were constant mild tremors here on the island of Kos, this was much more violent than usual. James was thankful they hadn't yet begun the operation.

"Please bring the child back to consciousness and wheel him outside," he requested of the anaesthetist. "Everyone please leave the building and go outside to safety," he told the rest of the staff. They evacuated the building and all stood together on the land surrounding the centre.

The earth continued to move, but the tremors soon began to subside. James and his staff remained outside in case there were any aftershocks which might significantly affect them.

When it seemed like it had settled, they went inside to see if there was any damage. They'd been lucky and only found a couple of trays had fallen to the floor and some of the toys had fallen off the shelf and lay scattered on the floor, but there didn't seem to be anything more. Fortunately the centre had been built in line with building regulations regarding earthquakes, as Kos lay on a plate which stretched from Turkey.

They discovered that the epicentre was between Turkey and Kos, and with Kefalos being at the far side of the island, it had sustained little damage. Kardamena had suffered slight damage but Kos town had borne the brunt of it, with damage to many buildings in the town centre. A minaret had fallen across the square and a large dome had moved on its plinth.

The quake had caused a huge wave to form in the harbour, sending water about a metre high through the streets and restaurants close to the sea front, and actually sinking or damaging boats moored in the Marina. A large crack appeared along the harbour front.

James offered his services immediately, in case anyone had been hurt or trapped in any buildings. They were to learn sadly that two people had lost heir lives, but fortunately all other injuries sustained by the people in Kos town were minimal. For days afterwards there were continuing slight tremors, whilst the Teutonic plates settled again until next time.

People talked about the possibility of it having disturbed the magma flows beneath a sleeping volcano on Nissyros. Everyone had a tale to tell about what they had been doing when the quake hit, but apart from the visible scars at the harbour and in the square in Kos town, it soon became yesterday's news and life continued as normal.

Ohi Day

Every October the children at the schools on the island practised marching, ready for the parades on the 28th October. Although they prayed for good weather, some years their prayers were not answered and they'd had to march in torrential rain.

Whilst at school, these children were taught about the history of Greece and about the country's turbulent times during the Second World War. They learned poems and songs about those times.

The Ohi, or 'No Day' celebrations were to commemorate the rejection by the then prime minister, Ioannas Metaxas, of the ultimatum made by the Italian dictator, Benito Mussolini, on the 28th of October 1940, to allow Italian troops to cross the border into Greece. He responded in French, which was then the diplomatic language, "Alors c'est la Guerre" or "Then it is war."

In the following hours the Italian army entered northeastern Greece. The Greek soldiers and resistance movement successfully fought the invading forces and pushed the Italian-Albanian forces back into Albania.

Because of this, Hitler's German army had to step in, and so invaded Greece in April 1941. This occupation lasted until October 1944.

Word spread of this refusal and Greeks took to the streets shouting, "Ohi." At the time, in a national newspaper it was written, "Today, there is no Greek who does not add his voice to the thunderous OHI OHI."

Winston Churchill was noted as saying, "If there had not been the virtue and courage of the Greeks, we do not know what would have been the outcome of the war. Hence we will not say that Greeks fight like heroes, but that heroes fight like Greeks."

The 'Ohi' day parades and flag flying represent the bravery, solidarity and heroism of the Greeks during this war. It became a public holiday, commemorated with parades and with public buildings decorated with national flags. Schools and all places of work are closed to celebrate on the 28th of October.

When this day was celebrated in Kefalos, all the village children dressed in white shirts would march through the village, with the streets lined with clapping and cheering people waving flags.

This year, the village committee had chosen Grace to be the standard bearer and lead the procession. This was a great accolade to the little girl, the daughter of James and Caitlin, as they chose someone who was a good village resident and had helped the community.

As she marched proudly, the smile never left her face during the entire procession. James and Caitlin were so very proud of their daughter. Grace had far exceeded all of their expectations when she was born as a Down's syndrome child and had now become a true member of the Kefalos community. Everyone loved her and Grace was very happy living here in Kefalos.

As James and Caitlin grew older and their thoughts turned to Grace's life expectancy, they were reassured that if they themselves were no longer here, then Grace would be well looked after and provided for, should she outlive them.

As the years went by, Grace began, and continued to work at the paediatric centre as a receptionist. She loved her job and enjoyed being a part of the team. However, although she'd become quite an accomplished individual, it was thought that independent living would never be the best thing for her. For this reason, James arranged for a one storey building to be erected on the land adjoining their villa. This was to become Grace's house, where she was helped by a carer to carry out daily domestic activities. Despite this, it still gave her a real sense of independence.

CHAPTER 7
SUZIE

Suzie, the eldest daughter of John and Jenny was an English rose through and through, a country girl with country habits and hobbies. She'd been brought up by her parents, along with her brother and sister, at the family home on the moors.

There had always been an abundance of dogs and horses for as long as she could remember, and Suzie had been involved with horses from a very early age, building a special relationship with her father's horses when just a toddler.

She was bought a small pony at a very early age, which she quickly learned to ride. Soon she'd competed in, and gained many first prizes at local competition in classes such as Bonny Pony, First ridden and Clear Round Jumping.

Hit by the bug she soon began show jumping, competing most weekends and travelling the length of the country to attempt to qualify for Wembley or Olympia. Her mother or father, Jenny or John drove her and her horse to the venues in the horsebox. Both parents were insanely proud of all her achievements. Countless rosettes were won and pinned on the wall in the tack room, where trophies bedecked the shelves of the display cabinets.

It was obvious that a career with horses was her ideal occupation, but she first decided to pursue a career in teaching. She enrolled at the local college and it was here where she met Daniel, the young man whom she fell in love with and subsequently married.

When John, her father became ill, her world fell apart. She had always been his little girl, in much the same way that Laura had always been Mum's baby girl.

Suzie was overcome with grief when he died, and although she held it together until after the funeral because she wanted to support her mum, she later became very distant and insular. Daniel suggested a grief counsellor and after a few sessions, she began to accept what had happened and began to plan her future life again.

She specialised in teaching children with special needs and later attended a college to qualify in all areas of horse management.

When Laura, her younger sister graduated from university, it was a surprise for all the family when her mother arrived from Greece to attend the graduation ceremony. It was a surprise because she was accompanied by an extremely good looking Greek man who told all the family it was his intention to marry their mother because he loved her.

Now Suzie was preparing to go to Kefalos to attend her mother's wedding.

It was the first time Suzie had visited Kefalos, but like James, she'd seen all the plans and photos of the house which their mother and father had built in Kefalos. She too had also been reluctant about her mother going to live there alone after the death of her father, but here she was, now travelling to Kos to attend Jenny's wedding to Yiannis, the Greek man she'd met and fallen in love with.

Suzie was pleased for her mother, and happy she'd once again found happiness.

The airport was busy today. They sat for some time waiting for the electronic board to tell them to go through to passport control and the baggage collection and checking area.

Daniel, her husband, seemed much more relaxed than her. They'd all met Yiannis at Laura's graduation, and even though they'd only spent a short time with him, they all agreed he seemed a good man and they all approved of their mother's choice of future partner.

At last they were requested to move to baggage check. Suzie always panicked at this stage in case she'd mistakenly put something in her hand luggage that wasn't allowed, however, today they passed through quickly and problem free and headed straight into the duty free area of the departure lounge.

Daniel found a seat near the bar while Suzie went to buy a small personal gift for her mother. She chose a tiny sky blue heart on a silver chain.

"Something blue for the bride to be," she said out loud to the checkout girl, who looked at her strangely.

It was strange to think of her mother as a blushing bride, but she loved the thought of this ceremony making her mother's happiness complete.

Soon they boarded the plane and were on their way. She had much to see when she arrived at the destination, and much to organise as chief bridesmaid. Being the elder daughter, it was her responsibility to help Jenny prepare for the wedding. She was excited that she would get to see the house her father had commissioned to be built, the house which had been her mother's home for a short while, but now she knew her mother and Yiannis had built a home where they would live after the wedding and very much .hoped she would also get to see that house.

Shortly after take-off they were served a snack. Daniel seemed to relish his, but Suzie just picked at hers. She was looking forward to sampling something sumptuous from the Greek cuisine which her mum had always talked about.

It had been an easy flight, and when the plane did begin its final sweep out over the sea and then returned low over it, she gazed at the blue water and the high mountains near

Kardamena, with the hotels scattered in its shadow and up its steep slope.

The plane came to a halt quite close to the airport building, so it was surprising to both her and Daniel that they had to board a bus to take them the few yards to the entry of the arrival lounge and passport control. They passed quickly through to the baggage area and then attempted to find their luggage, which Suzie hoped hadn't been lost as it contained her bridesmaids dress and headdress. Mum had already arranged bouquets for her and Laura.

They searched through the waiting taxi drivers until eventually seeing 'Suzie and Daniel' written in large letters on a clipboard. They approached the driver and he helped Daniel with the luggage.

Suzie smiled. Finally they were on their way to Kefalos. The taxi driver spoke good English, probably from years of ferrying people to and from the airport.

"Your mother asked me to pick you up and take you to your hotel. I too am from Kefalos, so I know the man your mother is going to marry. He's a good man and well loved by the Kefalos locals," the driver said. Suzie was quite moved to hear this.

"That's really reassuring to hear," she told the driver.

"On the day of the wedding I have been booked to take you to the harbour, where you will catch the boat to the island where your mother will be married." He remained quiet for a few seconds and then went on to say, "Your mother told me you have never been here before."

"No, but I'm really looking forward to seeing everywhere she's spoken about," Suzie replied.

"You will love it here," the driver said, making Suzie smile.

For some strange reason, she was getting butterflies about seeing her mother after such a long time. James had told her how beautiful Kefalos was and how he and Caitlin had also fallen in love with it.

As with all Greeks, the taxi driver was very proud of this island and was always happy to talk about the beautiful beaches, the neighbouring islands and historic sites, particularly in Kos town.

Suzie and Daniel listened to the spiel as the man drove crazily along the main road known as the M1, which stretched the entire length of the island from Kefalos to Kos town, with most of the main resorts either a left turn or a right turn from it.

Eventually, after a pleasant drive past all the sights, they'd been dropped at the hotel and were now waiting for a phone call from Jenny to give them directions to the restaurant where they were going to meet later. Eventually the call came and they made their way to meet Jenny and Yiannis, and what a fabulous reunion it was.

"Hello my Darling," Jenny gushed as Suzie walked through the door.

"Hello Mum," Suzie said, beginning to weep.

"Now, none of that," Jenny ordered. "This is a happy occasion."

"Sorry Mum," Suzie replied, beginning to raise a smile.

Now, the countdown began. There were only two days to go before the wedding.

It was a beautiful day for the joining of Jenny and Yiannis. They enjoyed a wonderful wedding service for such a very joyous occasion, with everyone having an amazing time.

Suzie thought Kefalos was wonderful. She loved the Greek people, the food and the local lifestyle. She knew that she would visit the island many times over the coming years, eventually bringing her two daughters Maisie and Mia with her. They would also learn to love Kefalos too.

When her sister, Laura married a Greek named Nikos, a man she'd met and fallen in love with on the island, Suzie's daughters were the bridesmaids.

Soon after she and Daniel were married, Suzie discovered she was expecting Mia, and quite soon after this, Maisie was born.

Suzie put her dreams of a career on hold and became a full time mum until her girls started school. She then found work in a local school for children with learning difficulties. She saw how she could combine her love of horses and her expertise with special needs children, and it became her dream to open a riding school which would offer riding for the disabled.

Eventually with hard work and the help of her husband, Daniel, they bought a small farm, and with lots more hard work they converted it into a riding centre, where along with their own horses they offered stables for rent, riding lessons, and also therapeutic riding sessions for the disabled.

Mia and Maisie were involved in the running of the centre. Maisie, being so like her mother, loved her life working with horses, but Mia wanted more and was not so keen.

Mia - A Holiday in Paradise

When James picked up the phone, he was surprised that it was his sister on the line.

"Hi James," Suzie began. "What do you think about my daughter, Mia and her friend coming out to stay in Kefalos for a couple of weeks?" she asked her brother after a few pleasantries had been exchanged.

Both girls were aged seventeen now and would soon be starting university. James thought it was a great idea, but admitted he had little experience of teenage girls.

"I think it would be better for you to speak to Laura," James confessed.

The two chatted for a while and James assured her their mother was fine, and that her sister was totally engrossed in the Greek lifestyle. "You should try it, Suzie," he suggested.

"I would love to," Suzie replied but then continued, "but my life at the riding stables is so busy at the moment, there is not a spare minute in the day."

When the phone call ended, James smiled to himself. With two teenage girls let loose on Kos, he was very glad they were not his responsibility.

Suzie did as James had recommended and she phoned Laura to ask what she thought.

"I will find them accommodation down in resort, rather than staying with Nikos and me, or James and Caitlin," Laura told her sister, Suzie. "This will give them their independence. They don't want us oldies cramping their style," Laura laughed.

This was a great idea of Laura's, as it would have been a long walk to the beach from either of their villas. It was also better to be in a hotel in the resort to be closer to the nightlife the girls would enjoy,

Of course their uncle and aunty would invite them to their villas to have a barbecue and to swim in the pool, but they all knew how teenage girls preferred their own company, rather than that of older relatives.

Mia was keen to show her friend Jackie all the places which she'd visited many times with her parents, as well as the places and people that had now become special to her, almost like an extended family.

Laura had booked them into Sydney hotel, where she knew there was entertainment provided, live bands and the like. It was also a hotel where many younger patrons stayed, people who enjoyed the later bars and attractions, whilst the oldies had left to go home to sleep!

Both girls were thrilled with their room and within minutes of Laura dropping them off, changed into swimwear and had gone to the pool at the rear of the hotel to catch the remaining rays of the day's sunshine. It felt quite secluded here, with only a few sun loungers around the pool and a lovely dining area under a canopy.

It was amazing how much they had to talk about, even after having just chatted for over four hours whilst sitting next to each other on the plane journey. They'd listened intently as Laura spoke to them during the journey from the airport to Kefalos, and as usual, talked about the various beaches. This was Mia's first holiday without her parents, after which she would return to England to finish her final examinations at college.

"I'm trying to get the results I need to go to University," she told her Auntie Laura. She intended to cram as much enjoyment into this holiday as possible, in readiness for a period of intense study.

Laura and Nikos joined them in the evening, along with Dimitris, Toula, James, Caitlin and Grace, and they all enjoyed a family meal together.

On the instruction of Laura's older sister, Suzie, Laura laid out some ground rules for the holiday, to which they agreed and everyone seemed to be happy.

Mia and her friend, Jackie's holiday would begin properly the next day. This is when they felt their real freedom would begin.

They rose early and went down to the tables surrounding the pool to have a delicious cooked breakfast, which would set them up for the day. They decided to go and visit Cavos Beach near the harbour today. They settled themselves in the sun, put on their sun cream, as suggested by Auntie Laura, and had called into Kefalos market to buy sun hats and sunglasses. There were only a few people on the beach, so they had a choice of sun beds.

The girls tentatively dipped their toes into the water and felt the tingle of the chill of the water. The sea was very calm today, with only a few ripples on the surface. Mia told Jackie that she would take her to another beach later, where the sea was warmer and the waves were fantastic for splashing about in. The girls found Cavos Beach a little quiet today, with not too much talent to spot!

After a morning at Cavos Beach, they decided to take a walk up to the other end of Kamari Bay. The beach took them past Bravo Bar and Corner Cafe, and they noted these and added them to their itinerary for a future visit. They arrived at the windsurfing area of the bay, and here it appeared there were more people of their own age. Soon they were chatting to the young boys there who paid them a lot of attention, which was fun.

Tomorrow they would walk to Paradise Beach, which Mia knew was far busier than here, with lots of water sports and many more young people to mix with.

When they returned to Kamari Bay beach the next day, the boys they'd met at the surf centre were there and came across to chat. Mia and Jackie welcomed their company, and together they had a day full of fun and laughter. They arranged to meet the lads again during the holiday.

Uncle Nikos had promised them a sail on the yacht, and so Mia asked him if they could bring along a couple of friends. Nikos said it was fine as there was plenty of room.

"The more the merrier," he smiled.

Mia was excited to be able to invite their newest acquaintances, Chris and Tim to come with them today for the trip on the yacht.

The lads' eyes were opened wide as they stood on the harbour and spotted it, as the black yacht came round the headland and made its way towards them in the harbour. It was not too busy around the harbour today as the pleasure trip boats had already left, which made Nikos's yacht look even bigger!

Nikos sailed the yacht skilfully into the right side of the harbour and secured it to the Caxton with ropes. Chris and Tim were in awe of the beautiful black yacht with its reflective surface which seemed to change colour when it was viewed from different angles.

When the girls had spoken to the boys and asked them, "Do you fancy a sail around the coast?" they never imagined it would be on such a vessel as this.

"Uncle Nikos," Mia said. "These are our new friends, Chris and Tim."

"Pleased to meet you," Nikos returned smiling at the lads. "Welcome aboard."

They stepped inside the cabin and sank into the luxurious seating. Although they were a little subdued at first, Nikos soon put them at ease with his good natured banter.

"Can I ask what you do for a living?" Chris asked the obviously rich Greek.

"We run a family business working with boats," Nikos told them whilst winking at Mia. This made her smile, because although he was very modest, she knew he was a very rich man with an incredibly profitable business. Mia liked Uncle Nikos, because in her terms he was normal.

"Okay you lot, where shall we go?" Nikos questioned the four.

"I think that would be very much up to you, Sir," Tim said politely.

"Please, its Nikos to my friends," he stated. "And any friend of my niece, Mia, is a friend of mine," he smiled at the two lads, instantly putting them at ease. "Okay," he continued. "We will sale across to Nissyros," he announced.

Nikos piloted the yacht skilfully into the Harbour at Mandraki on the island of Nissyros, where they disembarked.

"Would you like to visit the volcano?" he asked, and everyone nodded in agreement.

Even here in Nissyros it seemed that Nikos was well known and well liked, judging by all the people who said hello to him and shook his hand. Because of his mobility problems, having had a below the knee amputation a few years back, he arranged for one of his friends to take them to the volcano.

When they finally arrived, it was not at all what they expected. They'd driven up the steep winding roads up the mountainous area and were expecting to see before them a classic vista of a volcano, but were surprised to see that the crater of this volcano was down a steep rocky path. They scampered down the slope and onto the surface of the crater floor. It was hot and smelly here, and they could see holes in the crust.

They walked up to, and listened to the tour guide, known as Georgie to her friends, as she proved that the surface was hot enough to fry an egg. Photographs were taken before they scrambled back up the slope and went to the cafe for a quick drink. After this, they were returned to the harbour and to Nikos by his pretty friend. He'd waited patiently for them, sipping his frappe whilst shading from the sun in the little café.

Upon their return, Nikos sailed by the old granite workings and anchored so they were able to swim in the crystal clear waters. The sail back was a little choppy, but the yacht hardly registered the movement at all.

When they returned to the harbour, the boys thanked Nikos profusely for the trip in the yacht, and then they walked the girls back to Sydney's, where they arranged to meet Mia and Jackie later, before carrying on to return to their own accommodation.

All four of the friends had really enjoyed themselves. Today had been a good day and one of many wonderful experiences.

During their stay, Mia and Jackie had visited Kochylari Beach and watched the talented surfers riding the waves most days, and had swam or tried to swim in the crashing waves. Tonight they were going to pay a visit to the lively resort of Kardamena to sample the nightlife there, with its famous street filled with bars and with music blaring everywhere.

Their new found friends, Chris and Tim came with them. As the evening wore on they were all becoming a little worse for wear from too many drinks consumed.

"I need to go home," Mia declared.

"Me too," Jackie agreed.

"Too many Ouzo shots," Mia laughed, and they all made their way back to the quiet of Kefalos, agreeing to meet again the next evening.

The next day, now refreshed again after the proceedings of the night before, Mia and her friend Jackie were on their way to visit Kos town. They were dropped off at the bus station and found their way by following other passengers walking towards the main shopping centre.

They walked past the beautiful church and carefully manoeuvred themselves down the marble steps, where at the bottom they crossed over to the back entrance of what had once been the fruit market. It now sold many herbs and spices, dried fruits and a selection of honey and olive oil. The smell they experienced when entering he building was a wonderful mix of all types of heady aromas. They decided this would be somewhere to call in, on their way back to the bus station.

The front entrance of the market took them back to the main square, where restaurants and tavernas had their tables and chairs set out under large umbrellas. The sun during the summer months was very fierce here, and the surrounding buildings amplified the heat.

A cold drink seemed to be the order of the day, so the two girls sat outside the first bar they came to, where they were quickly met by a good looking and very smiley young Greek man, who began chatting to them.

"Hello girls. My name is Stavros," the waiter announced. "How may I help you today?"

"Can we have two diet colas please," Jackie requested.

"Where are you girls from?" he asked while taking their order.

"We are from England," Mia smiled.

"Where are you staying on the island?" Stavros questioned, returning with their drinks.

"Kefalos," Mia answered rather nonchalantly.

Both questions were answered with vague replies, as both Mia and Jackie knew these were questions this young man probably asked the tourists a hundred times a day, in the hope of a good tip.

Once refreshed, they began to explore. Streets full of shops ran in every direction from the main square. Some of these led down to the fantastic harbour, where there were pleasure boats as well as yachts belonging to the rich and famous.

Along this harbour road the restaurants and bars had waiters trying to get every passerby to come inside their establishment. It was a little intimidating for the two girls, so they traced their steps back to the main square and began a more organised stroll of the various streets.

This was really the tourist centre, where there were shops selling souvenirs, shoe shops and clothes shops selling the proverbial football shirts and t-shirts with different slogans on them, alongside traditional style Greek hats. They purchased a few bits and bobs from here and then went to visit the extensive ruins, now laid out like park areas. From there they walked around the castle on the harbour front.

This area was so different from Kefalos. It was a busy capital town, with visitors from many nations. Groups of people were being led by tourist guides holding up their clipboards for the people to follow, whilst directing their groups around places of interest. One of these places of interest was Hippocrates tree, where tradition has it that, Hippocrates, the father of medicine, sat beneath its branches while tutoring his students.

The girls both felt like they'd walked miles laden with purchases, so began to make their way back to the bus station, or so they thought. Many of the streets look the same and they had to admit they were lost.

"I think it's this way," Mia offered.

"I'm sure we've been down here already," Jackie replied.

They traipsed on and were beginning to get worried about the passing of time, thinking the bus service to Kefalos was only once every hour. They seemed to be in a more residential area now and panic was beginning to set in.

Eventually they saw sign posts saying, 'Market Square,' and they quickened their pace and headed in that direction pointed to by the sign. They were so relieved to finally come back to the bus station. With weary feet and aching arms from carrying their shopping, they boarded the bus bound for Kefalos.

They were lucky to get a seat as the bus was soon full, and passengers were now standing in, and filling the aisles, with the girls hemmed into their seats by the standing passengers. As the bus pulled out of the station, with parcels stacked on their knees, they began the journey back across the island.

Many of the German passengers alighted at the all-inclusive hotels, with more filling their places from the water parks and the many stops along the way.

The bus finally arrived at the harbour in Kefalos, where the girls disembarked and walked slowly and wearily back to Sydney's, where upon arrival they relaxed on their beds for a little while. However, being young and fit, they were soon refreshed, showering and preparing for an evening visit to the various bars and tavernas along the seafront.

Although Mia had enjoyed the boys company, when it was time for them to leave and return to England, she felt no real emotional connection with them.

She'd loved the time with the family, as well as meeting the various Greek people, people who she now regarded as her extended family. She smiled to herself when she thought – yes - it had been a summer of fun.

Sadly, the holiday was soon over. On the final day, Uncle James took them to the airport and waved them off. He loved his niece, Mia; she was a crazy kid and full of fun.

They'd seen quite a lot of each other over this fortnight and he was surprised how grown up she'd become since last they'd met.

"She has her head screwed on, that one," he said to Caitlin a little later. "I will miss her company."

Mia didn't know what it was about Kefalos that so entranced her. She'd travelled to many places with her parents over the years and a lot of the destinations she thought were more beautiful and picturesque than Kefalos, yet there was still a certain something about the place that pulled at her. Kefalos had got under her skin even before she'd been there on this recent visit, the first without her parents.

She was totally chilled from the moment her feet touched the tarmac at Kos airport. She felt safe there, and the local people always appeared to be happy to see her, remembering her from previous visits. They would nod and smile at her when she went into shops and tavernas, making it definitely feel like her second home.

Mia had seen how happy her grandmother was to be living there, and when her Auntie Laura moved to Kefalos, she also became a respected member of the community.

When Uncle James had moved to Kefalos with his wife Caitlin and daughter Grace, Mia became intrigued as to why he left a fabulous job and a luxurious home in England. In fact, why exactly did so many people return year after year and then many of them make their home here?

Her mother and father had visited many times and she'd gone with them. Although they loved Kefalos, Mia knew they would never move there. Her mother's life revolved around her horses and the stables they owned, but Mia knew in her heart, it was where she wanted to be and call home.

Was it just a dream for her to move to the island? If it was to become a reality, she would need to start planning for her future straight away. But for now, Mia had to complete her exams and pray for good results. Luckily her prayers were answered and she passed her exams with top marks. She thought carefully about what she really wanted to do as a career, and which subjects would help her achieve this.

She researched the various universities, looking at the prospectus they offered and decided on Preston Polytechnic, which offered a course on the subject she'd chosen to study.

She enrolled in a two year course in speech therapy, with practical practice in centres around the country. Before she enrolled she wanted to make sure there would be a job at the end of it.

Mia's thoughts now turned to the facilities at the special medical centre set up by Uncle Nikos, and run by Uncle James. She knew that Laura now worked there and that Grace had been given a job as a receptionist, so she put a proposal in writing to Uncle James

Dear Uncle James.

I am considering my chosen subjects at university and have become increasingly interested in speech therapy. I note that at your practise there in Kefalos there is no such role at the paediatric centre and was wondering if I pursued this subject, whether a post may become available in the future?

Mia

James had a laugh when he received Mia's letter. It was so formal, as if sent by someone he didn't know and not a much loved family member. He thought of the happy go lucky girl who'd holidayed so many times on the island and knew his niece had now also fallen under its spell. For a laugh he first sent Mia a formal response, in line with the original one received, but then added at the bottom -

I would be crazy to hire you, but as I am crazy, make sure you get your qualifications and we will set up an interview. I am sure you would like it here, so come and spend a few days with us so that we can all get to know you.

Love,
Uncle James

CHAPTER 8
NEW LIFE – NEW CAREER

Mia studied extra hard, often burning the candle at both ends and finally obtained the qualifications she needed. James was very proud of his niece's hard work and was thrilled to be able to offer her the post of speech therapist at the centre.

A starting date was organised and James found a little place for her to rent down in the resort, as he thought she would like to be close to the sea when she wasn't working. It was a small, one bedroomed traditional old flat roofed Greek house, painted blue and white of course, with a small garden. Most importantly for the young lady, it was only a five minute walk to the beach and the seafront tavernas.

Laura took Mia shopping to buy bed linen, curtains and kitchen equipment. Together they soon made it cosy, and then Mia put her own mark upon it. She was feeling happy now living on the island, and soon knew her way around the resort and village, feeling quite at home almost immediately.

After a few days of settling in and revisiting family and friends, it was time for her to begin work. From day one she loved it, but was glad she'd taken time to learn the Greek language with the intensive course she'd taken whilst studying back in England. To be able to speak and write quite fluently in Greek was now essential. However, it made some of the children laugh when she sometimes mispronounced words. It all helped with her building up relationships, and the children all came to love her very quickly.

She left work at the end of each day feeling she'd made the right choice in coming to Kefalos. Every day she loved living here more, she always had. Her dream of living here in Kefalos had become a reality.

She was always busy at the centre, even so, sometimes during her free time they would call her at a moment's notice to help a traumatised child who couldn't control a stammer, or was unable to speak at all because of some trauma in their lives, but Mia didn't mind this at all.

She loved building a child's confidence by forming a special relationship with them. Slowly, through play and singing, the child would overcome the stammer and learn to speak again. She felt such satisfaction from being part of the gradual improvement and eventual successful outcome.

Mia loved her life here in Kefalos. She'd learned to be happy with her own company. Most of her days were filled with children and work, whilst her evenings were about relaxing, sometimes with family, but often alone, although she never felt lonely.

She always kept in touch with her family back in England, contacting them by video call. She also enjoyed spending time with Laura's children, and James and Caitlin's daughter, Grace. She was an ideal babysitter for them all and she loved it.

She had no appointments that morning, so she ventured down to Kochylari Beach, but she was not happy with the sight that met her. The rough overnight winds had brought in the seaweed and the entire shoreline was bathed in the black mass of swirling tentacles. It looked so different from its usual flat sand beach which made it very popular with the tourists, as many beaches on the other side of the island were shale or pebble stone beaches in the Kamari Bay area.

It had been ruined today and looked like a disaster had struck! Many tourists pulled up in their cars but immediately drove away again. Mia felt sorry for the guys who kept the beach tidy and free from rubbish which drifted over from the island of Kalymnos. They were fighting a losing battle against nature. As they cleaned an area, a fresh wave brought in more black seaweed. They held out their arms up to the heavens, as if to say they'd given up!

Mia was quite happy to lie on the lounger and just enjoy the sunshine and gentle breeze, so different from the fierce wind of the night before. The gentle sound of the waves lapping provided a soothing lullaby, and soon she was drifting into a deep sleep. This was the paradise she'd left England for, and she loved it.

Meeting Sophia

Over the months, Mia had become a gorgeous dark haired beauty, so much so that with her olive skinned tan she now actually looked like a Greek local.

She sat in the garden of her little rented house, situated just off one of the smaller roads in the resort. She loved it for the independence it gave her and although it was basic, she had added her own personality to it.

Now in the height of the summer, with the school closed her appointments were greatly reduced. She was now able to enjoy the downtime after being so busy in the spring term.

She decided to venture out for a gentle stroll down to the beach. Putting on swimwear and covering it with a Kaftan, she grabbed a towel and began the five minute walk down the short road leading to the seafront.

She spotted an empty sunbed at the end of the row outside Bravo Bar, so fastened her towel on it with two giant pegs and then put on her sea shoes. Mia had learned over the years that the pebbles here were difficult to balance on or to get a secure footing whilst trying to get into the sea. She had laughed so many times at macho looking men falling over and pretending it was part of a dive into the sea.

She knew only too well the sea here was always a little chilled and colder than other places on the island but today it was welcome, as the overhead sun was fierce. After a refreshing swim, she completed the manoeuvre back onto the sand.

She noticed that the previous occupants on the sun lounger next to hers had departed and it was now occupied by a beautiful young Greek girl. Mia felt a strange, tingling feeling, when she watched the girl sleeping on the sun lounger. It was a feeling she'd never felt before but she was able to shrug it off.

After drying herself, she lay in the sun and tried to sleep but found it impossible. She couldn't take her eyes off the girl on the bed next to her. She wondered how old she was She thought she looked about the same age as her.

Mia glanced up and down her lithe body and again felt a deep feeling inside. She wondered what her name might be, because such a beautiful girl must have a beautiful name.

She watched as the girl awoke from her slumber, opened her eyes and caught Mia looking directly at her. Mia was mortified to think that she'd been caught staring at her, but the girl gave her a lovely smile which lit up her dark eyes. Mia just had to smile back in return.

"Did I make a noise in .my sleep? Was I snoring?" the girl asked, to which they both laughed.

"No, no, no," Mia replied, a little lost for words.

"My name is Sophia," the beautiful girl announced.

"Pleased to meet you, Sophia, my name is Mia," she confirmed.

'What a lovely name,' Sophia thought, 'a lovely name for a beautiful lady.' Mia's heart was beating so fast, what on earth was up with her.

"Are you from Kefalos?" she questioned.

"Yes. I was born here, but I've been to university in Athens for three years. Are you on holiday here?" Sophia questioned.

"No, I live here. I work at the paediatric centre in Kefalos," Mia informed the Greek beauty.

"I have seen you here on this beach before," Sophia confessed.

"I don't get much free time," Mia replied "It's very busy up there in the centre."

"I've got a lot of time at the moment," Sophia admitted, and then went on to tell Mia, "I've finished my studies now and must find a job. I help my mother; she rents apartments, so I've been cleaning the rooms for her until I can find a proper job."

"What did you study at university?" Mia asked

"Marine engineering," Sophia replied. Mia's eyebrows raised showing surprise. "I know," admitted Sophia. "It's strange for a girl, but I've always loved the sea, and adore boats and being on them."

"Perhaps you know my uncle Nikos. He builds yachts, well his company does," Mia revealed.

"Do you mean THE Nikos of Kefalos?" Sophia asked wide eyed. "It would be my dream to work for a company like his." Mia laughed.

"I'll have to introduce you to him," she said.

"Promise," Sophia requested and laughed. Mia noticed that her eyes sparkled when she did so. "Will you be here again tomorrow?" she questioned.

"I can be," Mia replied.

"Okay, let's meet here again tomorrow," the beautiful Greek suggested. Mia agreed and arrangements were made.

As Mia later walked back to her little house, a thousand emotions were running through her body. She'd never felt this way about anyone before, let alone about a girl. Was it right for her to be feeling this way? Meeting Sophia had sent chills of expectation down her spine. She felt almost overwhelmed by it all.

After eating very little that evening she went to bed early, hoping to dream of, well, she didn't know what to dream of, or maybe she did.

The next day, Sophia was waiting as arranged when Mia arrived at the taverna. She suppressed a smile at Mia, as if she was surprised that she'd actually turned up, but then she broke into a beaming smile when she realised that Mia looked very pleased to see her waiting there for her.

They sat with heads together, chatting about everything and anything, listening to each other's stories and learning about each other's families. It transpired that they liked a lot of the same things. Every so often, as they laughed about something, Sophia would touch Mia's hand or shoulder, just a friendly touch and quite normal, but each time she did this it sent a tingling sensation throughout Mia's body.

On another occasion when they met, Sophia seemed to hold on to Mia a little longer when she hugged when greeting her. Mia enjoyed this extended contact and wondered if it would be the same when they said their goodbyes. She hoped so.

They continued to meet after work, or on their days off, with both girls enjoying each other's company immensely. Mia's feelings for Sophia were now becoming more than just friendship. She fought continuously with her own conscience when she imagined really kissing Sophia and snuggling up with her. Yet she said nothing to the beautiful Greek vision of beauty, or to anyone else about these feelings she was experiencing.

Mia was now fighting in her mind about what her feelings were for Sophia. Were these feelings something she would have regarded in the past as something unnatural?

She liked boys and she'd had fun with boys, she'd even dated a couple in the past, but nothing had given her the sensations and emotions she felt when with Sophia.

After much soul searching, Mia decided she would distance herself from Sophia and tell her she wasn't able to see her. She needed this time out to really decide what to do.

To spare her feelings, Mia phoned her and told her she would not be able to meet her for a while as she had extra works prep to do, and this would take up all of her spare time.

Sophia seemed to accept this, but said a little sadly, "I will miss you so much, Mia, but I understand. I will be here for you when you have time to be with me again."

Mia wanted to cry, scream and shout when she finished the call. She sat on the bed with tears running down her face. Had she done the right thing, she wasn't sure? She did know she was hurting at the thought of not seeing Sophia again.

A couple of weeks passed and Mia began to realise that life without Sophia had no sparkle. She missed her terribly, and was now feeling miserable, alone and lonely.

She no longer took pleasure in her little garden, and work didn't seem to give her the buzz it normally did. She missed their time together and she missed the closeness, the touch of her hand and the smile on her face, which spread to her eyes and made them sparkle. She missed her crazy laughs. In fact, she missed everything about her friend.

Mia really needed to clear her head. It wasn't even light when she went out of the house that morning. There had been very heavy dew overnight and everywhere was damp, which heightened the fragrance of the gently wafting oleander and bougainvillaea bushes.

She deeply inhaled the scent as she looked up and saw that the mountain had a collar of cloud around it. This was early morning in Kefalos, before the peace and tranquillity was broken by cars and motorbikes carrying early workers to their places of work.

She wandered along the lane, this time away from the direction of the beach and along the back road past the Anthoula and Eleni hotels, following the road which joined the main road just past Zeus, and the Tea for Two café.

She carried on up the main road and past the entrance to Ikos, where she wandered up the incline past the vantage point where tourists stopped to take pictures of Kastri Island in the Bay of Kamari. She didn't even notice where she was actually walking, but just walked aimlessly.

She walked past the sign for Paradise Beach, one of the most visited and most talked about beaches on the island, then followed the sign on the main road that denoted Volcania Beach.

She trudged past the winery and finally reached the beach. It was deserted. Even the most diligent and determined sun worshippers wouldn't be here at this hour. There was an eerie bank of cloud shrouding the beach and completely hiding the island of Kalymnos.

She walked along the length of the beach towards the kitesurfing centre positioned on her favourite beach, Kochylari. The wind was getting up a little now and the breakers rolled in. She settled on one of the sun beds and sat there deep in thought for some time.

'I know what will clear my head,' she thought, and removing her shorts and t shirt and undressing down to her bikini, she waded into the waves. She felt a slight chill, but with each wave her body became more accustomed to the temperature of the water. It wasn't easy to swim here, but between breakers she attempted a few strokes.

Now she felt truly invigorated and could think more clearly now. Instead of jumping from subject to subject in her head, she made her decision. As she made the long walk back alone on the beach towards her home, Mia made the decision to confess to Sophia and tell her how she was truly feeling about her. She struggled with how to broach the subject and what words to actually say, as she didn't want to risk losing Sophia as a friend but needed their relationship to go further.

"Can we meet, Sophia?" Mia asked her friend on the telephone a little later. Sophia was extremely pleased, even excited to receive the request, and accepted.

They were sitting close together, just as they usually did. Sophia looked deeply into Mia's eyes when Mia took the plunge and began to speak.

"Please don't be offended by what I'm going to say, or the way I'm trying to express myself," Mia began somewhat awkwardly."I've had such a wonderful time since I met you, and have enjoyed every minute I've spent with you."

She stopped talking for a few seconds and looked at her friend to see if she could gauge any reaction. Sophia was looking at her with a confused expression on her beautiful face. Mia decided to bite the bullet, so she took a deep breath and went for it!

"Sophia, I have come to like you very, very much," Mia began.

"You like me?" Sophia questioned, looking strangely disappointed.

"Yes, I like you, "Mia continued. "But I have deeper feelings for you than just friendship. I think you should be aware of that."

"Please Mia, tell me about your real feelings for me," Sophia pleaded.

"Sophia," Mia stopped to compose herself. "I love you. I have never felt this way about anyone before and I am confused about the emotions that run through my body when I think about you."

"You love me?" Sophia said smiling. "Oh Mia, you don't know how long I have felt the same about you, but was afraid to say in case I scared you away. I needed you to experience what I was feeling, so that I could truly tell you how I feel."

"But I'm confused," Mia admitted. "I have never felt this way about a female before. Oh Sophia, you know what I mean," she said shyly.

"I know exactly what you mean, Mia," Sophia replied, trying to reassure her. "I discovered a few years ago that I found girls more attractive than males. I fought against it myself for a while, but I spoke to some gay friends who explained to me how they felt and how difficult it was for some people to admit they were gay."

"I'm gay?" Mia questioned, but then answered her own query. "I suppose I must be."

"I once met a girl who I liked a lot, so we began a gay relationship," Sophia continued. "It lasted about nine months, but then we decided to go our separate ways. For a long time now I have been single, but when I met you, well, I sort of knew that this might be a chance for me to find happiness again." As she said this, Sophia leaned over and kissed Mia on the cheek. It was a kiss of such tenderness that it brought tears to Mia's eyes.

"So what happens now?" Mia questioned, realising that Sophia was the far more experienced girl in this relationship.

"Depending on how you feel, we could take our relationship a little further, but one step at a time," Sophia instructed Mia. "I know it's all new to you, but you will gradually come to terms with it. Soon you'll want to tell your family and eventually your close friends and confess your sexuality to all. If they love you, and I'm sure they do, they will accept you for the person you have become," Sophia explained with great tenderness.

Mia couldn't believe what she was hearing, that it was okay to feel this way. Also the revelation that Sophia knew from the moment she'd met her that there was something special about her. Mia could not have been happier

"Now my darling, let's get on with enjoying life," Sophia announced. "And as the Greeks say, 'sigar, sigar' - slowly, slowly, until you are perfectly sure that this is what you really want."

As she heard the beautiful Sophia saying this, Mia already was sure that this is what she wanted.

Mia wandered down to the beach early on Saturday morning. As usual, it was deserted at this hour so she perched on one of the many empty sun beds and gazed out to sea.

The waves this morning seemed somewhat furious, with everywhere along the beach being filled with the white foaming sea. Mia was normally mesmerised by the motion of the sea, but this morning she'd come here to clear her head.

She had tossed and turned all night thinking about what Sophia had said, words which she'd welcomed, especially as her own feelings were so very similar. She wondered if it was just a passing fancy, but knew in her mind that it was deeper than that.

She desperately needed to talk to someone to see how they would react to how she was feeling about Sophia. It would be difficult talking to Mum over the phone about this, and she knew it would be quite a while before she could chat with her face to face.

She'd always been close to her Auntie Laura, who'd been like a surrogate mum to her since she'd moved to Kefalos, so Mia decided she would have a heart to heart chat with her. She rang and as usual, Laura was happy to meet up with her.

Laura wondered if perhaps she was a bit homesick, maybe needing a friendly face to talk to, or perhaps just a big hug to reassure her there were people here who cared for her and understood the pull of family in England.

Many times Mia went over in mind how she might bring up the subject of her sexuality with her auntie. They'd arranged to meet in Corner Café. It was almost empty when Mia arrived so she found a table away from the centre, where she felt she could talk freely without being overheard by anyone within earshot. Laura arrived promptly and greeted her niece in the traditional way, with kisses on the cheeks. She could see that for some strange reason, Mia looked nervous, so Aunty Laura decided to instigate the conversation.

"Right," Laura began the conversation with an air of authority. "What can I do to help you, Mia?"

"I'm not sure how to put this, but here goes nothing," Mia spoke quietly, almost in a whisper, even though there was no one in close proximity.

"What is it Mia?" Laura asked, now worried.

"I don't want to shock you, Aunty Laura," Mia began, "but I have met a Greek girl and she's lovely.

"That's nice dear," Laura replied, not yet understanding the situation.

"No, Aunty Laura, you don't understand. I really like her, I like her a lot. In fact I have very strong feelings for her, feelings unlike anything I have ever known, or felt before. This girl has told me that she feels the same way about me, and that she is gay." Laura looked at her enquiringly.

Mia had rushed all these words out and now paused for a moment to look for a reaction from Laura, but none came, so she continued.

"I feel that, NO, I know that this relationship is right for me, but Aunty Laura what do you think?" she questioned.

Laura looked deep into Mia's eyes and her reply pleasantly surprised her when she told the girl, "My dear, love is love in any form. Who is to say whether it's right or wrong, but if she makes you happy, then it makes me happy," she hugged Mia.

"Thank you, Aunty Laura," a relieved Mia returned, feeling like a huge weight had just been removed from her shoulders.

"Well then, do you have a photo of her I can see?" Laura smiled. "And what is her name and when do I get to meet her?"

Mia was a little taken back with how well Laura had reacted, but she was now feeling very happy and relieved. "Her name is Sophia," she told Laura, as she searched her phone for a picture of her new friend. She selected the best one and showed it to Laura.

"Wow!" Laura reacted. "She's simply beautiful, stunning, and so are you. You two look so good together. What a gorgeous girl your Sophia is."

'My Sophia,' Aunty Laura had said. Mia had never thought about Sophia as being hers, but she supposed she now was. She was overcome with emotion, not knowing what to say as tears filled her eyes. It hadn't been easy to reveal this to her auntie, but she could tell that Laura accepted it, just the way it was.

"How do you think Mum will react?" Mia asked.

"Much the same as me if I know your mum, she loves you very much and would want you to be happy, just like I do," Laura looked at Mia. "Come here give me a hug. Let's give your mum a ring. I'm sure she would love to hear from you."

"What now?" Mia gasped.

"Come on, Mia," Laura reassured her niece. "There's no time like the present. Strike while the iron's hot!"

The telephone conversation was a little awkward to begin with, but Mia soon knew that it was totally accepted by her mum, and it would be by the rest of the family.

"If this girl, what's her name, Sophia, makes you happy, then she also makes me happy. And I for one cannot wait to meet her," her mum, Suzie told Mia, and just like that all her fear and anguish had been taken away.

She could now go back to Sophia and tell her the good news. They could be together without any fear of prejudice or judgement. Life for Mia and Sophia was going to be great, beautiful and a life full of love, Mia was sure of that.

Sophia said she would take Mia to meet her family, but explained to her that they spoke very little English. Although Mia spoke very good Greek, good enough to help children lose their stammer, put her in the middle of a room full of Greeks all talking rapidly together, she would soon become lost in the conversation.

Sophia was an only child, unusual for Greek parents to have just one child but that's the way it happened, and this was the reason she was so precious to her parents.

She guided Mia down the narrow streets in the centre of the village, a labyrinth of streets and passages in Kefalos with rows of apartments connected to each other, all with only a small balcony outside or a front door leading directly into the street. She looked up to see lines of washing hanging overhead, where large terracotta pots on the balconies were substitutes for having no garden. She noticed some little shops were interspersed between the rows of homes, where ladies sat outside on the streets, all chatting whilst nursing babies on their laps.

It was a hot day and little air penetrated these streets. At last they reached a house where the front door opened onto the side street.

"Mama, Papa," Sophia called.

Sophia's mother came from the back room, wiping her hands on her apron. She smiled at Mia and held up her hands.

"Psomi," she announced.

"Bread," Sophia translated.

"Yes, I know," Mia stated. Mia had smelled the bread as she'd entered the house. It smelled both inviting and delicious.

Sophia shared a few rushed words with her mother, which Mia couldn't quite catch. Her mother then smiled at Mia, but as though embarrassed by her lack of English, she scurried back to the kitchen and continued tending to the bread.

Sophia held up her hands in despair. "That was my mother," she confirmed.

"She seems like a lovely lady," Mia said.

"Yes, she is," Sophia replied. She then called her father again, "Papa."

A tall man came through from the confines of another room and walked directly to Mia. "Kalos herete," he said, "Welcome."

Again, Sophia rushed out a few lines in Greek to her father and then turned her attention to Mia. "Papa, this is Mia, my friend," she instructed. Her father smiled and then returned to whatever he was doing in the other room.

"Well, Mia, that is my crazy family," Sophia laughed. "They expected me to be married by now with seven kids!" They both laughed at this.

"Tomorrow you can meet my family and I will introduce you to my Uncle Nikos," Mia said to her beautiful friend. Sophia's eyes lit up at the prospect of meeting a man whom she'd admired from afar for a very long time.

The introductions the next day were much easier with Mia's family than with Sophia's. Everyone was delighted to meet Sophia, the girl they'd heard so much about. Of course, this time the language difference wasn't a barrier, with them all speaking Greek and Sophia speaking perfect English. Because of this, it was easy to get to know everyone.

"So this is the girl who has been making you so happy?" Caitlin asked smiling.

"Yes, Aunty," Mia replied.

"Oh Mia, she is very beautiful," Caitlin added.

"Yes, she is," Mia replied. "Not only is she beautiful, she's also a wonderful girl."

Caitlin smiled when hearing her niece saying this. She could see that Sophia made Mia very happy, and that was good enough for her.

As for Mia, all the anxiety she'd been feeling before announcing her sexuality by telling everyone she was gay, had now completely disappeared. She smiled across at Sophia, and she nodded back to Mia.

"I told you so," Sophia mouthed to the girl who was now officially her girlfriend.

CHAPTER 9
FUTURE PLANS

The season was in full swing, with tourists from many countries flocking to Kos to enjoy wall to wall sunshine, beautiful beaches, Greek cuisine, and the very friendly and welcoming people of Kefalos.

With the school closed for the summer there were fewer appointments for Mia to deal with, so she was able to take time off to recharge her batteries and swim in the sea whenever she was able.

Nikos, always the best of employers had given Sophia a job with his company and was now graciously giving his new employee time off to spend with his niece. When he wasn't too busy, he would take the entire family out on the yacht, and this obviously included the new addition to the family, Sophia, as everyone had now accepted her into the fold.

These were crazy, joyous and noisy occasions, full of love and merriment. Their lives were so intertwined that there were very few days when they didn't see each other, either at work, or sharing an evening meal together.

Mia and Sophia had been living together for some time now in the little house which Mia rented down in the resort area. It was obvious to all that they were meant for each other.

At the end of each working day, they would walk down to the beach near Corner Café and swim in the sea there. After their swim they would warm up with a hot latte in the café before walking home. Sometimes they would eat there. Mia particularly liked the club sandwich whilst Sophia enjoyed the wonderful sweets and pastries they sold. The two agreed that life for them both was good.

One day after their daily swim, Sophia had a question for Mia. "How would you feel about us taking this to the next level and making a real commitment to each other?" she questioned.

"What do you mean?" Mia asked, although deep in her heart she had an idea what was coming.

"I mean, how would you feel about taking the plunge and actually getting married?" Sophia elaborated.

"I would be delighted," Mia smiled.

"So let's do it!" Sophia shouted and both girls screamed with sheer delight.

They talked about a small ceremony on the beach, close to where they'd first met. They pondered on how they could show they were actually married, perhaps by having a double barrelled surname. Mia's surname was Taylor and Sophia's was Kapiris, so it would have to be either Taylor-Kapiris or Kapiris-Taylor.

They tried it out on paper several times and even asked the family what they thought. In the end it was decided that Kapiris-Taylor sounded best, so this was added to the official paperwork regarding the blessing.

On the day of the ceremony the family erected an arch bedecked with flowers, on the beach as close as possible to where the two girls had previously met. Chairs were arranged in a semi-circle facing the arch, with the sea and the island of Kastri as a backdrop. It all looked sensational and it made a beautiful location for a wedding.

All the members of the families were there, including Mia's mother and father, who had flown over to see the marriage of their daughter. Sophia's mother and father came along too. They had accepted the situation after much explanation from Sophia, who told them that this was just a promise that the girls would remain together and would look after each other.

Both girls wore Grecian style long flowing dresses, and had garlands of flowers in their hair. Two young friends acted as bridesmaids, wearing emerald green Grecian style dresses.

It was a beautiful spectacle to see them standing together on the beach, and a glorious occasion when they repeated the vows to each other.

"Together we complete each other. Everything you are I love dearly. From the moment we met, I knew you were the person I wanted to spend the rest of my life with," Mia said, with Sophia grinning ecstatically.

"In a beautiful place, I met a beautiful girl who turned my life upside down. My heart was beating so fast when we first spoke. I have learned to love you more than I have ever loved anyone before. You are my world," Sophia said, with everyone in the congregation also falling in love with her.

After the ceremony, they all drove up to Laura and Nikos's villa, where a barbecue had been prepared around the pool. As usual with any family gathering, it was filled with joy, laughter and love.

Mia and Sophia were totally devoted to each other, but yearned for a family of their own. They considered options such as adoption, but it was difficult, being as Mia was a foreigner living on a Greek island. Although they had their residencies, the authorities were not forthcoming in considering them as suitable parents, so they spent many hours contemplating the options available to them.

Mia decided to speak to Uncle James, as he was not only a loving uncle but also a knowledgeable medical man with connections in the medical field. She went to see him in his office at the centre and explained how she and Sophia wanted a child of their own. They were anxious to try and arrange the use of a donor. James listened intently and could tell the two had thought long and hard about this.

"I know of a fertility specialist with a clinic in Athens," James revealed. "We speak quite often and I could ask if he could help."

"Would you please talk to him, Uncle James?" Mia pleaded.

"How could I turn you down," James laughed. "But I cannot promise you anything. Please don't get your hopes up, because I have no idea of the protocol of this. I don't know how it all works."

"Thank you so much, Uncle James," Mia said hugging him. "You're the best."

James could tell how much it meant to her and a few weeks later an appointment was made for both Sophia and Mia to attend the fertility clinic in Athens.

They flew to the mainland on an early morning flight, both very nervous with neither knowing what to expect. When they arrived at the clinic they were welcomed by the consultant.

"Come in please ladies. My name is Doctor Angelos. I am a good friend of your uncle, James, and anything I can do to help any member of his family would be both an honour and my pleasure," he said. This was very reassuring, particularly for Mia to hear.

They chatted for a long time about everything involved in the process, and they also listened to his every word. It was suggested by the consultant that he did a full medical check on them both, to see which of them would be the best to carry the baby.

Doctor Angelos gave them a list of tasks to complete, including regular blood pressure checks, menstruation sequences and general well-being. He took blood tests there and then to checkout any possible problems, and then scheduled another appointment for them to attend after they'd completed the required monitoring.

The girls attended the second appointment, where the results were reviewed. After much consideration it was decided that Mia would be the best of the girls to carry the baby. Now all they had to do was continue the monitoring and sending the results through to the consultant. He would get in touch with them when he felt it was the most beneficial time for conception.

When the call finally came, both Mia and Sophia were thrilled, but also scared at the same time. They flew to Athens and when they arrived at the clinic, Doctor Angelos was there to meet them. He carried out a few simple tests and asked a few more questions, and then smiled at the girls.

"Okay, Mia, if you're ready, we can get everything ready for you," he said calmly, making Mia feel instantly at ease.

He left them alone in the room whilst he went to prepare for the procedure. When he returned he led them to an adjoining room, where after a few more small preparations, Doctor Angelos was ready to continue.

"Can Sophia stay with me, Doctor?" Mia questioned.

"Of course," Doctor Angelos smiled. Sophia held Mia's hand tightly.

The little operation was performed more quickly than they'd anticipated. Doctor Angelos told Mia to, "Sit still and rest for a few minutes." He left the two girls alone and left the room. When he returned half an hour later, he questioned, "How do you feel, Mia?"

"I feel okay," Mia said.

"In that case, you are free to leave," Doctor Angelos replied, and the procedure was over. Hopefully the girls would discover that Mia was pregnant very soon, although Doctor Angelos had some sound advice for them upon their departure.

"Mia, please take things a little easily and let's see what happens," he suggested. "Don't get too upset if it doesn't happen on this first try, we can arrange to perform the procedure again."

"Thank you so much, Doctor Angelos," the girls said, thanking him profusely. They then left the clinic, where once outside they hugged each other for ages. They were so happy.

"Our baby might just have been conceived," Sophia said, almost laughing.

"Let's go and celebrate with cakes from our favourite patisserie," Mia offered.

"Cake, yes," Sophia stated jokingly. "But no alcohol for you, now you're an expectant mother," she laughed.

They couldn't control their excitement. Although they knew it might not happen this time, surely they would be lucky one day in the future.

Each day they looked at the calendar and put a large cross next to the date when Mia's period was due. Finally the day arrived, today was the day, but nothing happened. The next day, nothing happened. They held their breath as day three and four passed. Could they really be so lucky? On day seven they contacted the consultant in Athens.

"Wait another week and then come and see me," Doctor Angelos advised.

Each day they dreaded that they might be mistaken and Mia's period might begin. Each and every day they had more hope, but even more anxiety.

Finally, two weeks had elapsed and they again took the early flight to Athens. They went to the clinic to meet Doctor Angelos and he was ready for them.

"Did you bring a urine sample?" he asked.

"Yes Doctor," Mia replied. "I did as you said and took this at the first pee of the day," she said, handing the doctor a small container.

"Good girl," Doctor Angelos smiled. He then left the office taking the urine sample with him, and as he did, Mia felt terrified. She looked at her wife to see that Sophia also looked really stressed. It meant so much to both of them.

When the doctor returned to the consulting room, he sat down at his desk and wrote something on the paperwork in front of him. He then looked across the desk at the girls. His expression gave nothing away.

"Well my dears," he said eventually. "I hope you have the nursery ready because it looks like Mia is pregnant. She's going to have the baby you so much wanted."

Both girls broke down in tears. Even Doctor Angelos almost shed a tear to see such happiness in his office. Antenatal appointments were arranged, after which, the two flew back to Kos, smiling all the way.

"Pinch me," Mia said. "I think I've been dreaming."

"Well I must have had the same dream," Sophia returned and they both laughed.

They began attending antenatal clinics together, always going to the appointments as a pair. The day finally arrived when they had a very important and really exciting appointment. For today's appointment was for Mia to be scanned and they would get to see their baby for the first time with the ultrasound scan.

"This might feel a little cold," the nurse announced smiling at the expectant mother to be.

Mia climbed onto the couch and then the nurse applied Jelly to her ever expanding lump. Nurse Chrisoula turned on the screen and gently manoeuvred the monitoring device over Mia's belly.

The girls looked to each other. The screen at this time was turned away from them, but Chrisoula slowly turned the screen around.

"Look girls, there's your little baby," she said. She always enjoyed this part of the appointment, when she saw the joy on the parents faces.

Sophia and Mia both gasped as they saw the image of their little baby growing inside Mia. They squeezed each other's hands tightly.

"Do you want to know the sex?" Nurse Chrisoula asked. Both girls looked at each other.

"Do you want to know?" Mia questioned Sophia.

"Do you?" Sophia asked her back. Mia nodded, so both girls looked at Chrisoula, smiled and nodded. "Yes please."

"Well, get plenty of pink balloons," the nurse laughed. "It appears you're having a little girl. She's a good size and at this moment she's sucking her fist. Take a look."

The nurse pointed to the image on the screen. They were mesmerised by the picture which showed their baby really was sucking her tiny fist.

Two copies of the scan were printed off, one for each of them. They couldn't stop looking at the images as they left the consultation room, both on cloud nine.

"A little girl, how wonderful," Mia said, almost exploding with happiness. They were going to be a complete family and would have everything they ever wanted.

Before returning to the airport and flying back to Kos, they decided to splash out and buy a pretty outfit from one of the designer shops in Athens. They would have to decide about prams and cots and a whole load of things which they would have to buy at a later date, when back in Kos.

"I don't think Uncle James knows, but I know he does speak to his friend, Doctor Angelos, quite often. Perhaps we should call a family gathering. Let's get everyone together and tell them all at the same time," Mia said excitedly.

Mia telephoned her uncle. "If possible Uncle James, could you get the family round to your house tomorrow night for a family gathering?" she questioned.

"Of course I can sweetheart, and I'll tell Aunty Caitlin," James replied. He had an idea of what the meeting might be about, but kept it to himself.

Mia telephoned Laura. "Are you and Nikos able to come to James's tomorrow night, and bring Toula and Dimitris?"

"Of course, we'd be delighted, but why?" Laura questioned.

"Let's just say that Sophia and I have an announcement," Mia said mysteriously.

"Okay. We'll see you there," a confused Aunty Laura told Mia.

For the rest of the evening, Mia and Sophia sat in the garden just gazing at the image of their much wanted and already loved daughter. They both had their fingers crossed that everything would be alright.

The next evening at Uncle James and Aunty Caitlin's villa, both girls teasingly wore pink to the family gathering, but no one noticed, suspected anything, or commented. They gave out envelopes to each member of the family, and then gave each a piece of paper and a pen.

"Everyone," Mia announced, getting all the family's attention. "We want to play a guessing game. We would like you to write down what you think our surprise is, then put it inside the envelope and write your name on it."

Everyone did as they were asked. James winked at Mia and said he would collect the envelopes.

"There's a prize for the person who guesses correctly," Sophia told them with a grin.

Mia read out the suggestions, one said they were getting a new house, another, a new car, a trip to England, a special holiday.

"You're all wrong," Mia laughed, but there was one envelope yet to read and the name written on it was Laura's.

Mia tore open the envelope and read the contents in silence. She smiled when she showed it to Sophia and then to the rest of the family.

"Well everybody, Auntie Laura has guessed our surprise," Mia revealed, thoroughly excited about what she and Sophia were about to disclose. She unrolled a large photocopy of the scan and held it up to show them all. Everybody cheered.

"And the prize goes to Auntie Laura," Mia said. "She is the lucky person who has won first prize and will be the baby's Godmother." Everybody clapped at hearing this.

"What a lovely prize," an honoured Laura said.

"Do you mind?" Sophia questioned for conformation.

"Will you be our baby's Godmother, Aunty Laura?" Mia asked.

"Girls, I will be highly honoured to undertake that role," Laura gushed. "Thank you so much."

"This calls for a celebration," James declared handing out glasses and opening a bottle of sparkling wine. "Here's to the first new born of the next generation," he toasted. "Please raise your glasses."

"Not you, Mia," Sophia ordered. "You're pregnant."

Everyone laughed at hearing this, but raised their glasses anyway to congratulate the happy couple and new parents to be.

Jenny sat quietly, deep in thought. She thought about her first husband and how proud John would have been to see his children's children starting a family. She also knew how much Yiannis would have loved it too.

Sadly she was now the only survivor of that generation, but was proud to have been included in the celebration. But then it suddenly dawned on her.

"Oh my God!" she shouted. Everyone turned to look at her as she continued. "Everyone, I'm going to be a Great Grandma. I really must be getting old." When they heard Jenny saying this, everyone laughed and applauded the now old lady. Sadly it was not to be, as Jenny was never able to meet her great granddaughter.

CHAPTER 10
GOODBYE GRANDMA

James had tried several times to contact his mother that morning, but with no response. He became worried because she always rang him every morning to say she was fine.

When Yiannis had passed, much against the family's wishes, Jenny had stubbornly stayed at the remote house where they'd lived together. She'd always felt safe here, but her children were concerned that since Yiannis had died, Jenny had become much frailer and a bit of a recluse. This was the second time that she'd been widowed, but she felt blessed that she'd found love again with Yiannis after losing the children's father, John. Of late she'd become a little more forgetful, but was always happy to see her children and grandchildren.

James was unable to get to the house, as he was conducting an emergency operation assisted by Caitlin. He knew that Laura and Nikos had taken Mia, Sophia and the children to Athens for the day, so his only option was to phone the police. A short while later the centre received a call from the local constabulary, and with a great deal of anxiety, James came to the phone.

"I am very sorry Sir, but I have some bad news for you." James could feel his knees begin to buckle as the officer continued. "We couldn't get any answer from your mother, so we had to break the door down to gain entrance. We found your mother sitting in a rocking chair outside on the upstairs balcony. Sadly I have to inform you that your mother has passed away."

"Thank you officer," was all James could think of saying. He was numb, stunned about his mother's death. He then smiled to think she'd passed away sitting in her favourite chair overlooking her favourite view.

"Once again, I am very sorry to be the bringer of such sad news," the member of the Greek police offered. "But if it's of any consolation to you, when we found your mother she had the biggest smile I have ever seen on the face of a deceased person. She must have died whilst thinking very happy thoughts."

"Do you think she looked peaceful?" James questioned.

"Very peaceful Sir," the officer confirmed. This made James smile.

He cancelled all non-urgent surgery for the rest of the day and then telephoned Suzie at her home in England.

"I'll go to the airport and get the next flight," Suzie told her brother. She knew that Greek funerals were arranged very quickly, normally between two or three days.

Everyone gathered that evening in the home of James and Caitlin. They sat and chatted well into the night, reliving lovely memories of Jenny, their mother and grandmother.

They knew she'd loved living here in Kefalos and she always felt blessed that she had met Yiannis and learnt to love again after losing John, her first husband. She'd also loved it when first Laura, and then James had made their homes in Kefalos. And when her eldest grandchild, Mia, who was expecting a baby, now lived here with her partner, Sophia, she felt truly blessed.

Three days later, surrounded by her three children and five grandchildren, along with many of her Greek friends which she'd made over the years, Jenny was laid to rest next to her beloved Yiannis in a plot they'd purchased many years before, with its lovely views of their special cove. It was the perfect place for them to be together for eternity.

After the funeral, things slowly returned to normal. There were lots of things to do regarding Jenny's house. They needed to decide whether it should be kept, rented out or sold. Another decision would be what to do with the first house which John and Jenny had built together. Maybe one of the grandchildren would like it, since they were all living in rented accommodation. It would be ideal for Mia, Sophia, and for Jenny's future great granddaughter. It was close to the village and would be a good location, close to the paediatric centre for Mia, and close to Nikos's office, Sophia's place of work.

The house overlooking the cove, which had been Jenny and Yiannis's home, now stood empty. Yiannis had no immediate family, so it was up to them to sort out what remained of his possessions, as well as sorting their mother's assets. There were still some of her things in the basement at the first house overlooking the Bay of Kamari.

Here there were stacks of photographs of their mother with Yiannis taken over the years, wedding pictures and lots of family photos. James and Laura came to realise that in this house, Jenny's life with Yiannis appeared to have been a very happy one, but there was nothing of Jenny's life prior to this.

Yiannis had made James the executor of his will, and James had sorted all his affairs out when he died, with all his estate being left solely to Jenny, as he had no children of his own.

Yiannis had been a very wealthy man with several businesses which were subsequently sold, making Jenny a very wealthy widow, not that she cared about the money, she would have given it all away to have had Yiannis back by her side.

Now it was up to James and Laura to carry out their mothers wishes. The house was quite secluded and remote, and because of this, James wondered if they would struggle selling it, or renting it out, so hard decisions had to be made.

All the personal things were taken from one home to the other, where they had to sort out Jenny's possessions left in the basement when she married Yiannis and moved to the house overlooking the cove.

There was a collection of things tracing her life with John, items she'd brought with her from England when she'd moved there. Although these things were precious to Jenny, they had no real value to anybody else.

Again there was another pile of photos taken of the farmhouse they'd renovated, along with wedding pictures of Jenny's marriage to John and Suzie's wedding to Daniel, along with photos of their first two grandchildren. James also came across some lovely photographs of John and Jenny's holidays in Kefalos, with stage by stage photos of the construction of this house.

James and Laura sat on the floor wading through all the paperwork. Amongst the mementos, they found a tiny pair of pink booties with the hospital tag denoting Emily's birth, along with a picture of the tiny white coffin which held her body when she was laid to rest all those years ago. James and Laura both felt a lump in their throat as they viewed these items.

One box contained lots of John's personal possessions which Jenny had brought out with her. There were cards sent from well wishers when he was in hospital, along with condolence cards sent to Jenny when he'd died. Also in this box was the traditional rose, which all the family had kept in memory of John.

It was an emotional task for the brother and sister sorting through these things, because they were reliving the loss of their father, as well as their mother.

There were pictures of Sue, Jenny's friend and the girl who'd been inseparable to their mother during their teenage years. Sue had taken her own life at a very early age and James and Laura's oldest sister, Suzie had been named in honour of Sue.

There were, of course endless pictures of the three children, showing achievements at school and sports they were involved in.

There was ample storage space in the basement of this house to store these items, so they were repackaged and placed in sealed plastic boxes, although some items were sent back to England for Suzie.

When they returned to the house on the cove they placed fresh flowers on their mother's and Yiannis's grave. They stood in silence remembering what a lovely couple they were and how much they missed them.

Following discussions with all the family it was decided that Jenny and John's house would be gifted to Mia and Sophia. Mia was thrilled with this very generous present. The house, being close to the village and to all the amenities was in an ideal location for them, and they were soon able to move in and immediately put their own stamp on it. They began converting one of the rooms into a nursery for the imminent arrival of their baby daughter.

Jenny and Yiannis's house was near the beach, and although a little remote in its area, was an ideal summer house. It was felt each member of the family could use it, meaning that Suzie could come out with Daniel anytime they wanted.

All the family were happy that both houses would be in use again and not empty. They all knew that Jenny and John would have been extremely happy that the house they'd built for them would now be used by their great granddaughter.

CHAPTER 11
A NEW GENERATION

All the sun beds had been removed from the beaches and they'd been returned to how nature had intended them to look. The sea had removed any trace that any people had been there.

Though there was now a little chill in the air, Mia and Sophia decided to walk along the shore from Paradise Beach past where the bubbles appeared from the volcano, and on to Lagarda. No pirate ships or fishing trips were seen now, as the season had well and truly ended.

The beach stretched out in front of them, with Club Robinson perched on the jutting headland. The sun sparkled and danced on the waves, which were much bigger than in the confines of Kamari Bay.

They walked slowly along Marcos Beach and Sunny Beach, and then on to Magic and Exotic, a favourite spot for nudists. In the near distance they could see the buildings of Blue Lagoon Resort. They would only walk a little further today, as when they turned round they realised the distance they'd covered, with Paradise Beach now quite a way away.

They chatted as they walked along. It was getting more difficult for Mia walking on the soft sand, as her walking now had become a waddle as she was reaching her seventh month of pregnancy. Fortunately she was strong and healthy, and at every check-up or hospital visit she'd attended, the test results had been spot on, with Doctor Angelos being very pleased with her progress.

Nine months had seemed like an eternity. Mia continued working until the last month of her pregnancy, when the doctor advised that she should take some much needed time off work to rest.

Two days before her due date, Mia, accompanied as always by Sophia, travelled to the clinic in Athens and their favourite man in the world. Doctor Angelos was there to welcome them.

"How are you feeling, Mia?" the doctor questioned.

"I'm feeling like a beached whale," Mia replied, to which they all laughed, with Mia and Sophia's nervous tension being eased.

Very soon after their arrival at the clinic, nature decided the time had arrived. Before she'd unpacked her travel case, her waters broke and her labour began. Sophia held her hand, mopped her brow and whispered words of encouragement. In her own way, she felt every contraction her partner was enduring.

After a long eight hours, their baby daughter came into the world weighing three and a half kilos. She was a good size, perfectly formed and with jet black hair. She let out a resounding wail and then began sucking her fist; just like she had in the scan photo they'd been given.

The nurse went to pass the baby to Mia but she intervened. "Please give her to Sophia first," she requested. "I have been close to our baby for nine months, and now it's her turn."

The nurse passed the little girl to Sophia and her heart instantly melted. She was perfect. They finally had their own baby and their family group was now complete.

Such precious moments followed. Sophia and Mia took it in turns to feed their daughter and change her nappy. They took scores of photographs of the early hours of her life. They telephoned the family to give them the wonderful news and everyone was delighted for them. The girls had never been so happy in their entire lives.

Soon, after much deliberation they decided on a name. "So, it's settled, we are going to call her Kali," Mia said.

"Yes, because in Greek, the word Kali means good," Sophia agreed. Little baby Kali gurgled as if approving her mothers' choice of name.

A few days later, Kali was introduced to her extended family, as the first child of this generation. Everyone wanted to hold her and she was passed from person to person. She never murmured, being quite content to be held by all. Everyone agreed she was both beautiful and a welcome member of the family, who all instantly loved her. Mia videoed the celebration and sent a copy to her mother, Suzie, back in England.

The day they took baby Kali to meet her Greek grandparents it was a slightly different atmosphere. Although Sophia tried to explain that this baby was hers and Mia's, they shrugged their shoulders and looked at Mia.

"The baby's father has left you?" Sophia's mother questioned curiously.

"No Mama," Sophia replied. "Mia was artificially inseminated."

They didn't try to explain any further but Sophia told them that they would be 'Yaya' and 'Papoose.' - Grandma and Granddad to this little baby. This seemed to please them.

They took baby Kali home to their house, where, like all other newborn babies, she was spoilt day in day out by the devoted parents and extended family.

When Mia thought about her family, in her mind they were like invaders, slowly taking over a part of Kefalos and claiming it as their own! It was not like they'd created a ghetto or a settlement, but they just loved to live their lives living close to each other, so they could spend quality family time together. They'd become integrated and welcomed by the village inhabitants, and were well loved by many if not all of their Greek neighbours.

Mia looked down at Kali, who was growing up fast and becoming a mischievous toddler and now into everything.

She would start pre-school soon and to help, both mothers took it in turns to read to her in Greek and English. Sophia and Mia also ensured that they both spoke Greek and English to her so she was adept at changing from one to the other, whenever it was required. Mia thought it would be nice to have another baby in the house, but it wasn't particularly an easy option and they'd been so lucky to have Kali. Maybe it wouldn't be a wise decision to try it again.

James came to see her and Sophia one morning. "I have something to ask you, but please don't feel pressured in any way," he told them.

"What is it, Uncle James?" Mia questioned.

"We have a tiny baby born prematurely at the centre. The mother has abandoned it and we need foster parents once it has become more stable and able to breathe alone," James informed them, and then begged the big question. "I wondered how you might feel about taking on that task." Mia looked at Sophia, searching her face for answers.

She then asked the obvious question, "Not that it really matters, Uncle James, but is it a boy or a girl?"

"How stupid of me," James admitted. "He's a little baby boy."

"For how long would we foster the baby?" Sophia asked.

"Well that's the problem, I don't really know," James answered with honesty. "I have spoken to the authorities and it would seem that in the longer term, adoption would be the solution if the right parents could be found." Mia again looked at Sophia.

"So would we be considered as suitable foster parents or adoptive parents then?" Sophia asked.

"I have spoken about it to the authorities concerned," James revealed. "You were born here, Sophia, and have strong ties to Kefalos. Mia is seen as a perfect resident because of the work she does at the centre with children and their parents. Of course there is the usual bureaucracy attached to any adoption, but there doesn't seem to be too many obstacles."

Mia and Sophia both looked deep in thought, but had interested expressions on their faces as James continued. "However, the most urgent question is, would you be willing to foster in the short term, as I have to find a home for this baby soon."

Mia was absolutely delighted when Sophia said, "Well, if Mia is prepared to take this on, then so am I," she thought it would be wonderful to have a baby in the house again, and she was sure that Kali would love the idea.

They had several meetings with the various people concerned with the wellbeing of the baby, and this was even before they were allowed to see the boy. Eventually everything was finalised with regards to their approval as foster parents, so they went to meet the little boy.

The baby was still in an incubator, but he no longer needed the neonatal intensive care that he'd previously received. Mia and Sophia peered into the plastic cot.

"He looks so tiny," Mia said.

"Yes, and vulnerable," Sophia added.

One of the nurses came and lifted him out of the incubator, and as Sophia sat on a chair the nurse handed the little tot to her, carefully ensuring the oxygen supply was still close by should it be needed.

The baby stretched and moved about as Sophia cradled him in her arms. His eyes were beginning to open and as she stared at him, he seemed to stare back, with a little bubble forming at his mouth. It was clear to all that she'd fallen in love with him immediately.

Now it was Mia's turn. She held him softly as he squirmed in her arms and tried to suck his fist. "Look," she exclaimed.

"It's just like Kali did when she was first born." Everybody smiled.

It was evident to everyone that this baby would be loved and well cared for by these two mothers. They both felt sad as the nurse took the baby away from them and placed him back in the incubator.

"If it all keeps progressing as it is at the moment, I expect to be able to discharge the baby to your care in about a week or two," James happily told them.

"Can we visit, Uncle James," Mia asked.

"Of course you can," James replied. "You can visit anytime, but only by arrangement with the nurses. Maybe next week you can bring Kali to meet her baby brother," he smiled.

Over the coming days, full of hope and anticipation they both visited whenever they could; holding the baby and talking to him so he was becoming accustomed to hearing their voices.

Two days later, they brought little Kali to meet her soon to be baby brother. The meeting went well and Kali asked, "Can we take him home today Mummy?" She was so excited about her new brother.

It didn't take Mia and Sophia long to arrange a special bedroom just next to theirs, in readiness for the homecoming. Many of the items they'd kept from when Kali was a baby were still like new and were brought into the house. Finally, Mia and Sophia were called for the handover.

"We need you to name this baby," said the care worker. Do you have any thoughts or preferences?"

Mia and Sophia had not even thought about it, always referring to him as baba.

"Maybe you could name him after one of your fathers," the care worker suggested, seeing their indecisiveness.

"Daniel is not really a Greek enough name. He'll be brought up here in Greece, so he needs a Greek name," Mia suggested. "Sophia, what's your father's name?"

"Babis," Sophia replied and smiled.

"Well that's nearly the same we've been calling him, baba," Mia observed laughing.

And the last letter is not sounded in Greek when speaking, so the 's' is silent," Sophia advised. So 'Baby Boy' was to be Babis Kipiris-Taylor. Kali was delighted to have a baby at home. It made her feel quite grown up to be an older sister to Babis.

It took two years to finalise the actual adoption, but eventually he became a true member of the family. Kali was now at school and Babis was soon to go to pre-school. He was such a happy child, always laughing and smiling. He loved going to the beach as a family with Mia, Sophia and his sister, Kali. They all played in the sand and ran in and out of the sea.

Mia had started to work part time once Babis was able to go to his Yaya for some of the day, but she had to admit she missed the children terribly when not with them. Sophia was the same as Mia, and always rushed home to be with her little family at the end of each day. They would put their children to bed, singing songs and telling stories to them in both Greek and English. They were so happy with what life had handed out to them. Life for all the family of four was good here in Kefalos.

CHAPTER 12
MAISIE

Suzie's other daughter, Maisie, enjoyed her work at the stables, and like her mother, was an accomplished rider. She was now giving lessons to young riders after completing her training at college.

She visited Kefalos from time to time and found it enchanting. However, like her mother, her roots were firmly based in England.

Maisie still travelled to horse shows where she competed in showing classes and jumping classes, but didn't need her parents to drive her now as she'd learned to drive the horsebox herself.

Being quite competitive, she loved nothing more than to beat the competition, especially those riding horses which were much more expensive than hers. Today she was competing in jumping classes and had managed to qualify for two jump-offs.

Some of the other riders she knew quite well, having competed against them many times before, however, today she noticed a new rider was also in the jump off. She stood at the side of the ring holding the reins of her horse whilst waiting for her turn to jump. As she did so, she watched as a rider, unknown to her, entered the ring. He was very good and jumped every jump well, getting a clear round in a very fast time.

Maisie's competitive streak kicked in, and when she was called into the ring, she knew his was the time to beat. Looking at the ring, she planned where she could cut corners and save vital seconds. She kicked her horse on and 'Lucky Star' motored around the ring at breakneck speed, also finishing with a clear round. She'd made it in a mere two seconds faster than the mystery rider.

When she was in the line up to collect her rosette and trophy, the mystery rider was next to her in the second place position. He acknowledged her win by nodding to her, but then left the ring.

Maisie found herself scheduled to repeat the challenge in the next jump off, and intended to beat him again.

"Come on Lucky," she whispered in the horse's ear. "Come on girl."

Once again she cut every corner and asked her horse to take risks to again save time. She had another clear round in a very good time indeed. The mystery man entered the ring and Maisie's heart was beating fast. She wasn't usually so keyed up about winning, although she always did her best to finish in first place.

He rode fast and furiously round the ring, clipping one fence but the pole didn't fall so he also went clear. When the steward announced his time, he'd beaten Maisie by exactly the same time as she'd beaten him in the earlier jump off – two seconds!

In this line-up he took the first position and Maisie moved her horse into the second slot. She nodded to him and he nodded back. Once trophies and rosettes had been handed out, the riders did the traditional winners trot around the arena and then left.

Maisie took her horse back to her horsebox and settled him in with hay and water. She then went to the refreshment tent to have a drink and a bite to eat before the journey home. As she sat down on the refectory type benches, she noticed someone looking at her. To her surprise the young man stood, came towards her and sat opposite, bringing his drink with him.

"Well ridden," he said, complementing her.

"Well ridden yourself," she replied smiling, to which he smiled back.

"I know your name is Maisie," he remarked. "I'm Damon."

"That's a Greek name," Maisie pointed out.

"Yes I'm from Greece," he confirmed.

Maisie looked more closely at him and could now see the unmistakably traditional dark hair and features associated with the Greek race.

"Apart from my mum and dad, all my family, uncles, aunties, sister and cousins live in Greece," she informed the good looking young man.

"Really, where do they live?" Damon asked.

"On the island of Kos," Maisie replied.

"Wow, that's spooky. I'm originally from Kos," he replied.

Maisie wasn't sure whether to believe him or not, but it did make a good chat up line and she was enjoying his company, so continued to chat with the good looking Greek.

"Where on the island do they live?" Damon questioned Maisie.

"Kefalos," she returned.

"No" he exclaimed "That's where I was born. My family moved to England when I was ten years old. I have just graduated from college here."

"Congratulations," Maisie remarked.

"Thank you," Damon replied. "May I ask you, Maisie, what made your family move to Kefalos?"

"Well it started with my grandmother. She went there first when my Grandfather died and after a while, she met and married a Greek man and made Kefalos her home," Maisie began, and then continued to tell Damon the complete story about her family history in Kefalos.

After listening intently to the history lesson, Damon queried, "That's so amazing, but why do you not live there?"

"My mum and dad still live here in England. We run a stable yard and riding school, which I love being a part of, and it would take a lot to make me leave that behind," Maisie told him.

"Where is the riding school?" Damon asked.

"It's in Hamshaw," she replied.

"That's about ten minutes from where my parents live, but ours is just private stables where I keep my horses," he told her, almost in disbelief of what she'd told him.

They talked a little longer, but Maisie could see the light outside beginning to fade. "I need to make tracks soon," she said, almost apologetically. "I'm not keen on driving in the dark."

"When are you at the next show," he ventured to ask.

"In three weeks from now, I'm at Liverpool," she confirmed.

"I'm competing there too," he smiled.

"Perhaps I'll beat you again," she laughed.

"Ditto," he said, and then began laughing too. He then made a suggestion. "Maybe we could meet up before then, if you like?"

Maisie had really enjoyed chatting with him and thought it might be fun to see him away from the horse world.

"Okay I'll give you my number and we'll arrange something," she said, hurriedly scribbling it down on a scrap of paper. Damon seemed happy with the arrangement and this pleased Maisie, so they both left feeling happy.

She smiled as she drove home thinking it had been a good afternoon all round, and meeting Damon had been a real bonus. It was good to meet someone who, like her, was heavily interested in horses, which up until now had been the love of her life. She wondered if he would keep his promise and phone. She hoped he would, as she would really like to see him again.

She'd only been home a short time when her mobile began to vibrate. It was an unknown number, so she was about to reject it until she saw it was a local number.

"Hello," she said tentatively.

"Hi, it's me, Damon. Are you home safe and sound?" he enquired.

"Yes," she told him. "The roads were quite quiet."

"Yes I know," he told her.

"How do you know?" she asked suspiciously.

"Because I followed you most of the way home," he laughed. "Are you free to go for a drink tomorrow afternoon, being as it's a Sunday?"

Maisie took a deep breath. She had butterflies in her stomach. She wanted to shout, 'Of course, when, where?' However, she held back and controlled her emotions. Finally, trying not to sound too eager, she said, "Tomorrow? That's a nice idea. You can pick me up if you like. I can show you around our stables."

"Sounds good to me," Damon agreed.

"Shall I give you directions?" Maisie asked.

"No need, I've already Googled it," Damon said, almost apologetically. "Sorry if that sounds a little creepy." Maisie couldn't help laughing at him.

"What time?" she proceeded to ask.

"I will be there about two-ish," was his answer.

"Okay, sounds great," Maisie agreed.

"See you tomorrow, Maisie," Damon confirmed. "I'm really looking forward to spending time with you."

"Me too," she managed to say without sounding too excited at the thought.

She was up bright and early the next morning, ensuring all the chores were done and she was able to leave enough time to shower and change.

Promptly at two o'clock in the afternoon a little red sports car arrived at the main gates. Maisie checked to make sure there were no loose horses about and then pressed the button. The electric gate opened and let Damon inside. He got out of the car and Maisie gave him a conducted tour of the stables. He seemed quite impressed with the set up.

"Thanks for that, now how do you feel about going for afternoon tea and cakes?" he asked her.

"I would love that," Maisie replied.

"Okay, hop in," he commanded, opening the door for her.

Maisie signalled to one of the stable boys to say they were leaving and he opened the gate for them.

Damon took Maisie to a little tea rooms up in the Lake District. It was beautiful there. They were served with sandwiches, quiche, cakes and scones, with all the food being delicious. They then went for a stroll together along the edge of the lake, where they chatted nonstop about how they'd come to be involved in horses.

Damon spoke fondly of Kefalos. He told Maisie he went there every year to see his childhood friends and relations, and said how he visited and swam in the sea at his favourite beaches.

"I love it there," he smiled. "I think I would like to return and live there maybe, one day."

"I try and visit at least once a year," Maisie reported. "It really is a wonderful place to holiday."

After a lovely afternoon together, Damon drove Maisie home. When they arrived, he stopped off to meet Maisie's mother and father, who were busy in the stable yard.

"Very pleased to meet you," Maisie's mother, Suzie said. They chatted for a while and her mum was really impressed when Damon spoke of his early years living in Kefalos, and the fact that he still had friends and family living there.

After saying goodbye to 'Mum and Dad,' he asked Maisie if they could they see each other again before they competed against each other at Liverpool.

"I would be very happy to," Maisie smiled. "I had a lovely time today." This was music to the young man's ears.

After this first day they began to see each other regularly, both in the horse ring and at the weekends when there wasn't a show. Sometimes Damon would call round in the evening and help with the stable work, just so he could spend time with Maisie.

"Now we are seeing each other frequently, Maisie, I would very much like for you to meet my mother and father," Damon informed her.

This made Maisie very happy to think he felt this much of her, but it also made her a little apprehensive. She really hoped they would like her as much as their son obviously did.

Wanting to make a good impression, Maisie spent a lot of time getting ready for the meeting and choosing more conservative clothes than normal. Damon came to collect her and after a quick ten minute drive he pulled up outside an old manse style house, with ivy covering the front face of it. Parked outside the house were two, what Maisie would have called 'executive cars.' The cobbled courtyard led to a block of stables at the rear of the property.

"This is where my horses are kept," Damon announced.

Damon left his side of the car and came around to the passenger side, where he opened the door for Maisie. She straightened her dress as she got out. 'Here goes nothing,' she thought.

Damon showed his guest into the lounge, where both his parents were waiting. They stood and crossed the room to greet Maisie, hugging her in the traditional Greek way.

There was a very large painting over the fireplace, which Maisie instantly recognised as Kastri Island in Kefalos. Also in the room was a watercolour of the village of Kefalos, perched high on the hill.

"My mum painted those," Damon said, as he noticed Maisie looking at the pictures. "She likes to paint, and they remind her of her home."

"They're very good," Maisie observed. "She's a very good artist."

"Do you like Kefalos?" Damon's mother asked. Damon had already told his parents that many of Maisie's family now lived in Kefalos.

"Oh yes," Maisie affirmed enthusiastically "I've been to the island many times."

"I was born there and so was Damon's father. We lived there for many years until my husband's work brought us here about fifteen years ago," Damon's mother said.

"You have a lovely home here," Maisie commented, looking around the room.

"Thank you so much, but I miss the sea and the sunshine, neither of which I get much of here," she commented. "Do your parents live in Kefalos?" she asked.

Once again, Maisie told Damon's parents a brief history of her family, beginning with her Grandma Jenny and continuing until present day.

"And how about you, do you not want to go to live there one day?" his mother asked. "I know Damon would love to return there one day"

"Enough interrogation, Mother," Damon smiled.

"She's beautiful, Damon," his mother told him as she went into the kitchen with her son to prepare some drinks.

"Yes I know, Mum," he replied winking at her, which made her laugh.

Damon was no longer the wild child he'd once been. Mother was happy he appeared to be settling down at last.

Maisie had been left in the lounge with Damon's father. She studied him from across the room and found he was a good looking man. She could see how Damon took after him. Mother and son returned with frappes and a selection of Greek sweets, all of course lovingly baked by a real Greek cook.

Things relaxed a little as they got to know each other. Damon's mother recounted tales of how cute he'd been as a child and how they managed to get through the dreaded teenage years. Inevitably the family album came out, and Maisie looked at the dark haired toddler sitting astride a Shetland pony, who then later became a leggy teenager on a pony, a pony he was fast outgrowing.

There were lots of pictures of his horses with rosettes pinned to their bridles and Damon proudly sat astride them bolt upright in the saddle, wearing a huge and wide grin.

They chatted about Maisie and her horses, and about the stables and riding school. By the end of the evening, she felt she'd known them both for ages.

"Come again soon," Damon's mother shouted, as she waved goodbye, after which, the two both relaxed on the journey returning to Maisie's house.

CHAPTER 13
HOME AND AWAY

When Maisie had turned twenty-one, her father had arranged for one of the outbuildings to be converted into a house for her. There was a cosy lounge with a wood burner, a traditional fashioned kitchen with a Belfast butler sink and an Aga cooker, which also heated the entire house. There was one large bedroom on the first floor with built in pine furniture, along with a bathroom and toilet.

She loved her little home, as it gave her independence and space from Mum and Dad. Damon loved to sit here with her, and even imagined them living together in this little house.

As spring turned into summer, Damon told Maisie he was going to visit Kefalos. "Would you like to come with me, Maisie?" he asked.

"What a wonderful idea, I would love to go with you," she beamed.

They both arranged time off from their work. Suzie was more than happy to let Maisie go, as she'd worked really hard at the stable yard so she deserved a holiday. Maisie let her family in Kefalos know that she was coming to visit, but didn't tell them about Damon.

"You can stay here with us," Laura offered. "We have a room for you." Maisie gladly accepted the offer. Damon arranged to stay at his grandmother's house, but they planned to spend most of their time together.

When they arrived at Kos airport, a taxi was waiting to take them to Kefalos. The taxi driver came forward and hugged Damon, who began a much animated chat with him.

"I went to school with this guy," he excitedly explained. He introduced the driver to Maisie and he seemed to study her for a few moments.

"I know you," the driver claimed. "I've seen you in Kefalos with your family."

"You've seen me before, really?" Maisie questioned. They say Greeks never forget your face, Maisie thought.

"You have stayed here many times I think," the driver, Christos questioned. Maisie had to admit that she had, and that she knew her family were well known in Kefalos.

Christos then said something in Greek to Damon, to which he reacted. "You didn't tell me your family worked in Kefalos in the paediatric centre," he said. "I have met them," he stated.

It was now going to be easier for Maisie when she introduced Damon to her family.

She turned her attention to Christos and gave him directions for Aunty Laura's villa.

"I know," the driver smiled, obviously knowing where he was going.

When they arrived, Laura came out to meet them. Damon got out of the taxi to get Maisie's luggage and to meet her aunty. Being a Sunday, all Laura's family were there and they engulfed them both with hugs.

"I can make my way to my grandmother's house from here," he told his friend, whilst removing his bag from the taxi.

"We should meet up for a drink one night whilst you're here," Christos suggested to Damon, before slamming the taxi door and driving away.

They walked inside the villa and to her surprise, the rest of her family were all there with their children. Damon was introduced to all, being involved in so many introductions.

"This is my Uncle Nikos," Maisie said," My cousins Toula and Dimitris, my Uncle James and Auntie Caitlin, and this is their daughter Grace, another cousin of mine." By now, Damon's head was already spinning!

Next to come forward to be introduced was Maisie's sister, Mia. She hugged Maisie so hard she couldn't breathe, and then she did the same to Damon.

"This is my partner, Sophia," Mia proudly announced. "And this little tot in the pram is Kali."

Being of Greek descent, Damon was not at all overwhelmed by the meeting of so many family members. His Kefalos upbringing had been like this, and each time he returned to the island he received the same welcome.

After the initial madness, they went out to the terrace next to the pool, where Laura had prepared salads and mezes. Damon fitted in so well, changing from the English language to Greek frequently and with ease. As Maisie watched him, she had a real feeling of pride. She had grown very fond of him during the past few months.

As the day was quickly turning to evening, Damon spoke to Maisie. "I must leave now, Maisie, I need to go to my grandmother's house. I'll come for you in the morning, if that's okay?"

"Of course it is," she confirmed.

"Now go and enjoy your family," Damon ordered, to which Maisie looked him and smiled.

Nikos offered Damon a lift, but he declined, saying it really was only a short walk to Granny's house.

Maisie watched him walking down the gravel path to the main gates, where he stopped, turned around, and waved goodbye to her. At that very moment, she sensed her feelings for Damon were growing much deeper. She returned to the mayhem of her family, but soon asked if it was okay to retire.

"It's been such a long and tiring day, also a little emotional," she said. "I really need to get some sleep now."

"Of course, sweetheart," Aunty Laura smiled. "We have lots of time with you yet."

Maisie slept soundly in the beautiful room which her Auntie Laura had prepared for her. The next morning, she woke bright and early and went outside to sit on the terrace, where she enjoyed the early morning sunshine along with the wonderful fragrances coming from the many flowers in the garden.

An hour or so later, as promised, Damon arrived in a somewhat battered little car, so different to the beautiful red sports car he drove in England. She grabbed a beach bag, said her goodbyes to the family and they were off to spend the day together exploring this beautiful island.

"Okay, which is your favourite beach?" he asked.

"It has always been Kochylari. I just love the warm water, soft sand and the waves there," Maisie replied.

"What say we go there and see how it is today?" Damon suggested.

When they arrived, this normally beautiful beach was today plagued with seaweed.

"It's okay," Damon offered, seeing the disappointment on her face. "I'll take you to a different beach."

Damon drove to the airport and took the road down towards Mastihari. He took a right turn down a winding lane that led past the large all inclusive hotels and on towards the Lido water park. Almost opposite here he turned left, following a sign that said, 'Tam Tam Beach.'

He parked the car and they took the path through the dining area of the restaurant and down a planked walkway that led to the beach. It was a narrow stretch of sand with large waves crashing in, much like those on Kochylari Beach. The island of Kalymnos could clearly be seen from here.

They found themselves a sunbed and after leaving their bags on it, stripped off to their swimming attire and walked hand in hand into the foaming waves. The sea here didn't feel cold so they stayed in for some time.

Damon seemed to be watching Maisie's every move. After she splashed the water at him, he quickly swam towards her and ducked her head under the water. She resurfaced, laughing and choking at the same time. He put his arms around her and they stood in the sea kissing, totally oblivious to any other people on the beach.

"I don't know about you, but I'm hungry," Damon announced a little later.

"Me too," Maisie admitted, so they went to the outside dining area and ordered Greek salad with fried saganaki, washed down with fresh orange juice.

After a lovely day together, they drove home and Damon reluctantly dropped Maisie off at Auntie Laura's house. He so wanted to be with her every hour of the day and night.

It seemed everywhere they went in the village and surrounding areas, people knew Damon and were delighted to see him and meet Maisie. The people of Kefalos had always been welcoming when she'd holidayed there before, but this was a different level of friendliness.

Damon said he needed to call at his grandmother's house, so after driving to the village, he pulled up outside a small stone built house on one of the many narrow streets. Maisie was a bit nervous about meeting Damon's grandma, hoping she would approve of her grandson's girlfriend. Damon unlocked the door and beckoned her to come in inside.

Inside, the house was not anything like Maisie had imagined, as it was not decorated or furnished for an older person, but was very modern and bright. Maisie waited to be introduced whilst Damon busied himself collecting a few things he needed. He then turned to Maisie?

"Ready?" he questioned.

"Is your grandmother not here?" she queried. "Will I not be meeting her today?"

"I sincerely hope not," Damon told her. "She died several years ago." Maisie looked shocked as he continued. "I've always known it as my grandmother's house, so I still call it that. It's actually my house now, as I inherited it when she died and left it to me."

"So no approval needed then," Maisie said with a sigh.

"Anyway, now I've got you here, let me show you around. This is the lounge, through there is the kitchen with the door out to the little garden, and here is the bedroom," Damon said quietly, almost in a whisper.

He paused a little before entering and Maisie felt his hesitancy. She also hesitated, for she knew that stepping through the door to this bedroom today would take their relationship to whole new level.

Damon offered his hand to her and she took a hold of it. He led her inside the bedroom and to the bed, where he sat her down and then sat beside her.

"Is this what you want?" he asked, looking directly into her eyes with his heart beating rapidly in anticipation of the reply.

"I think it is," Maisie replied breathlessly.

Ever so slowly they undressed each other and slipped beneath the bed sheet. Damon caressed her body, kissing her neck and breast. Maisie groaned, and as he looked up at her, she smiled. They had both wanted this for such a long time. They were both adults, but they'd both been nervous of such a commitment. Gently, Damon made love to her, his beautiful girlfriend. After their lovemaking, as they lay in each other's arms, breathless and drained of all energy, Damon tenderly kissed her as she drifted into a wonderful sleep, full of happiness and contentment.

Every day after this, after they'd been to the beach or into town, they returned here to shower and make love. Maisie reluctantly returned to her aunt's house each night and eagerly awaited the next day, which she would spend again with Damon.

The holiday finally came to an end. Sad goodbyes were said to all the family, as well as new friends she'd made in Kefalos.

"Back to reality," Damon said sadly, upon touching down in England.

"Kefalos is just a dream again," Maisie added.

"It certainly is," Damon agreed.

"I think this time I left a little bit of my heart in Kefalos," Maisie admitted. Hearing her saying this, Damon smiled. It was just what he hoped would happen.

CHAPTER 14
SOUVENIRS OF KEFALOS

The next morning when Maisie woke, she pulled open the curtains and saw the rain falling. The skies were overcast, grey and very gloomy!

"I bet it's not like this in Kefalos," she cried out loud.

She soon adjusted again to life at the stables and went back to enjoying giving lessons, eventually putting Kefalos out of her mind.

One particular day, when Damon called to see her he was looking truly excited.

"Can you spare me a few minutes? I need to ask you something," he shouted across the yard.

"Give me five minutes. Let me finish this stable and I'll be with you," she shouted back.

After completing her work, Maisie went to look for Damon and found him sitting on a bench near the paddock. As she came closer, he grabbed her hand.

"Maisie, I am bursting to tell you this," he said without pausing for breath. "I've been left stables and a riding school by my uncle, as he knew I loved horses as much as he did."

"Wow! How fabulous," Maisie smiled. She could see how excited he was about it.

"There's more," he gushed. "It's a very profitable going concern and it will be enough to support me, but I can still do my present job remotely." He couldn't keep still as he told her this.

"That's great," Maisie said, joining in the excitement. "And where are the stables?" she queried.

"That's the bonus," he replied, and then paused before he told her. "They're in Kos. What do you think?"

"What do you mean, what do I think?" she said, a little puzzled by his question.

"It's a great opportunity for both of us," Damon revealed.

"How do you mean?" Maisie said feeling a little confused.

"We would run this riding school together," he told her.

"In Kos?" she asked in disbelief.

"Yes, and they want me to take it over immediately," Damon stated, still really excited.

"In Kos?" she asked again.

"Yes, that's what I said, it's in Kos," Damon had expected her to be happy about the prospect.

"But I can't move to Kos," Maisie said apologetically.

"But why not, Maisie, why can't you move to Kos?" Damon pleaded, somewhat bewildered by her reply.

"Because my life is here," she tried to explain. "I'm taking on more and more here at the riding school and it will eventually be mine, so I can't leave." Damon looked completely deflated.

"But you love Kos," he stressed.

"Yes I love Kos, but I also love England, and I love my lifestyle here," Maisie told him.

"I have to take this opportunity," Damon said. "I want you to come with me. We can get married there. I have to go in a couple of days to sort things out. Come with me, please," he begged.

He just couldn't understand Maisie's reluctance to accept this opportunity for them to be together.

"Damon, honestly, I cannot take any more time off right now. We are so busy here it's impossible, I'm sorry," Maisie was adamant, and Damon just had to accept that the wonderful dreams he had for them were just that - dreams.

"Please Damon, I love you very, very much, but you're asking me the impossible," she begged. "Please go to Kos and sort things out. Make the life that you want out there. It's still your dream to do that, but it doesn't include me."

Damon was heartbroken. He hoped he could maybe persuade her when he came back, once the transfer and legal things had been sorted. He had no more time left now, as he was off to Kefalos in two days.

Maisie buried her feelings and thrust herself into her work. She was feeling extremely hurt and upset at losing Damon, and began to note how tired and tearful she felt at the end of each day, and how sickly she felt when waking in the morning.

Her mother had noticed how lethargic she now was, but put it down to the ending of her relationship with Damon, so she didn't question it until one morning Maisie was uncontrollably sick when walking the horses in the yard.

"Time to see the doctor, I think," Suzie advised, becoming more and more worried about her daughter's health.

"I'm okay, Mum," Maisie argued.

"But you aren't," her mother insisted. "Come on. I'll make you an appointment."

Maisie began to consider as to how she'd been feeling, thinking it was just an emotional reaction to missing Damon. However, suddenly she had another thought. It was three months now since she'd been in Kos with Damon.

"Oh my God, I could be pregnant!" she cried out loud.

The doctor confirmed it. She was three months pregnant, which all added up. Maisie was unsure whether she should tell Damon, but decided he had a new life in Kefalos that didn't include her, or a child. He'd only returned briefly to see his solicitor here in England, and had returned immediately to run the business on the island.

She discussed the situation with her mother. "Should I tell Damon?" she asked her for guidance.

"That's up to you," Suzie told her daughter. "That has to be your decision."

"Mum, he asked me to marry him and move to Kefalos," Maisie revealed.

"And why didn't you?" her mother asked, astonished by this revelation.

"How can I leave you here with all this work at the stables?" Maisie stressed.

"Well you won't be able to do any work if you're having a baby," Suzie pointed out. "I have no problem with you continuing to live here and bringing your child up here, but you have to consider your future, and I believe that is in Kefalos."

"Really Mum, you don't mind?" Maisie questioned.

"Of course not, Darling, we love you and it's no problem to us," her mum said, but then asked an obvious question. "Now, are you telling Dad or shall I?"

"I'll tell him. Do you think he'll be okay about it?" Maisie asked, looking a little worried.

"If you were sixteen and telling him this, he would be upset. But you're a grown woman and you can make your own decisions," her mum reassured her. "But go gently when you're telling him. You're still his little girl."

Daniel, her father, was quite pragmatic about it when she told him. He simply hugged his daughter and said, "It's another blessing, Darling, another grandchild."

Many times Maisie picked up the phone to ring Damon, but she couldn't. She thought about messaging him –

'HI, HOW ARE YOU? - I'M PREGNANT'

No, perhaps a hand written, personal letter would be a much better option.

Nothing seemed like the right thing to do, because she didn't want to ruin Damon's life or make him feel guilty for abandoning her, not that he could take any blame as she hadn't told him! No, she was better keeping quiet and dealing with the pregnancy herself.

Maisie was now in her eighth month and was quite large, finding it hard to manoeuvre or walk easily. She found herself rushing to the toilet every five minutes, and if she sat down she would often fall asleep and then wake up really stiff, unable to get herself out of the chair!

She was fed up and wanted it over now. Her feet and hands were swollen and her clothes were like vast tents. She felt miserable, fat, and worst of all, she felt unloved.

Early one day she was wandering around the stable yard and treating each horse to a lovely fresh carrot when she heard a car coming down the lane. She didn't recognise the car, so she waited until it had reached the main gates. When it did, she had a pleasant shock. To her utter surprise, it was Damon.

As he got out of the car, he couldn't help but notice the very large bump invading her body. As he looked at her, no words came! He was in a state of total shock!

He looked her up and down and searched her face for some kind of reaction. "Maisie?" was all he could muster.

Maisie looked at him patted her growing lump. "Your souvenir present to me with love from Kefalos," she announced.

Damon didn't respond at first, he just opened and closed his mouth several times but with no words coming.

"Why didn't you tell me?" he finally pleaded, as suddenly the tears ran down his face.

"What difference would it have made?" she remarked, a little too sarcastically. "You have your life in Kefalos, whilst my life is here."

"But it's not the life I want," he admitted sadly.

"But it was your dream to live there in Kefalos," she reminded, with more than a little edge to her voice.

"Yes, but with you!" Damon confessed. "As it is now, I'm not happy there. I need you there with me, Maisie, I miss you so much."

Maisie felt a lump in her throat. She'd been very emotional of late and the slightest thing brought her to tears.

"I have missed you too," she had to admit. Before she could move, he threw his arms around her.

"We need to be together," Damon said. "I will leave Kefalos and move back here. We can bring up our child here, together as a family."

"But that's not what you really want, is it Damon?" she said knowingly.

"Not quite," he admitted, looking a little guilty. "I still want to marry you and for us to eventually live in Kefalos as a family."

"Then I will stay here and take care of our baby alone. I'll tell it what a wonderful man its father is," Damon looked completely downtrodden.

"We need to sit and talk," he pleaded, and that's exactly what they did, for hours.

He told her he would not return to Kos until after the baby was born, and true to his word, he made arrangements for his staff back in Greece to maintain things until he returned. Every day he came to see Maisie, and at the end of each day he returned to his mother's house.

The baby was now overdue, with Maisie looking tired and bloated. Damon held her hand as she waited to find out what the obstetrician had planned to do with her.

"I think we will need to induce you," Doctor Thomas finally said. "The baby is a good size, so the sooner it makes an appearance the better."

Maisie was admitted to the antenatal ward where a drip was fitted to a cannula on the back of her hand. The magical substance dripping into her soon had the intended effect. She began to have proper contractions.

Damon never left her side. This was the woman he wanted to marry and the mother of his child. Maisie was simply his world. To this young Greek, nothing or no one else mattered.

A healthy baby boy was born into the world and both parents wept tears of joy. Damon proudly held his new-born son in his arms.

"Welcome little one" he whispered as he kissed his tiny forehead.

Maisie looked on at this precious moment. Oh how she loved Damon and how much she really missed him when he was in Kefalos. How she longed for the loving relationship they'd shared here in England before he left for the island.

She watched him again as he cradled his son. She could see the love he had for the baby was oozing out of him. It was written all over his face. They talked about a name for their little miracle.

Custom has it in Greece that the first son is named after the paternal grandfather," Damon suggested. "My father's name is Alexander." Hearing this made Maisie smile.

"Alexander was my grandfather's second name," she revealed. "We must tell all our parents now."

"I haven't told my mother and father yet," Damon said.

"Then you must tell them they have a grandson, and his name will be Alexander," she smiled.

There were so many calls to make, all answered with shrieks of disbelief from all the family in Kefalos, as unbelievably, no one there had been told about Maisie's pregnancy. There would be many celebrations on the island tonight, welcoming another new member to the family's Kefalos dynasty.

Damon drove Maisie and Alexander home. The delighted grandparents popped in just to say hello to their new grandchild, the first boy and a new cousin for Kali.

"Hello Alexander," Suzie gushed. "I'm your grandmother."

Damon continually gazed at Alexander whilst holding him in his arms. He sat trance like for what seemed hours, without taking his eyes of the newborn.

"I love you, and I love this present you have given me," he said to Maisie tearfully. "I want you both to be part of my life, and for us to be together in Kefalos," he beseeched her. Maisie smiled and their little boy gurgled.

"Perhaps," Maisie said. "Who knows?" She hugged Damon tightly.

CHAPTER 15
IMPORTANT DECISIONS

Maisie sat down with her mother. Alexander was fast asleep and her father was somewhere in the stable yard. Damon was currently in Kefalos ensuring the riding school was up and running, and ready for the start of the coming season.

"Mum, Damon wants me and Alexander to move out to Kefalos to live with him," Maisie coyly announced. "I'm not sure if I can leave you and Dad behind."

Suzie thought hard before she replied, but then said, "Look Darling, I know that if you move to Kefalos, I will miss you and Alexander, and I'll especially miss seeing him growing up every day, but I will visit you as often as I can," Suzie told Maisie. "I like Damon and know he will take good care of you and the baby. I also know my grandson will enjoy a much better life in Kefalos, surrounded by his uncles, aunties and cousins."

"But," Maisie tried to butt in, but Suzie was having none of it.

"But nothing, my girl," she said sternly. Yes, I will miss you but I will understand. This has to be your decision, and whatever decision you make I'll support."

"Thanks Mum," Maisie said to her lovely mum, but was still unsure of her decision.

"Whether you decide to live here, or in Kefalos, you definitely have to be with Damon," Suzie stated. "Also, think of Alexander and the life he could have there in the sunshine. Think of his cousin, Kali, and how lucky she is to be able to play on the beach and swim in the sea every day, with the lovely weather for most of the year."

"But Mum, you have always known that although I love Kefalos and adore visiting the island, I have never had a desire to live there before," Maisie claimed.

I know dear," Suzie responded. "But Kefalos has been planted in your heart by Damon. It's your life, Darling, and you must follow your stars."

Maisie gave her mother a big hug. She had a big decision to make.

A few days later, as she sat feeding baby Alexander, she looked closely at him. His dark hair and olive skin was an obvious reminder of his Greek genes. Maybe he should be brought up in Greece. She still pondered over what her mother had said to her, but was still unsure if it really was what she wanted to do.

Deciding she needed another viewpoint from someone who had actually moved to Kos and married a Greek, she placed Alexander back in his cot, took the plunge and rang her Auntie Laura.

"Yassou," Laura answered in Greek. Maisie was a little taken aback, as her Greek was quite limited.

"Auntie Laura it's me, Maisie," she said

"Oh sorry, force of habit. Most phone calls I receive are from Greeks," Laura laughed. "How are you, and more importantly, how is baby Alexander?"

"We're both fine," Maisie mumbled.

"Not a very convincing, reply," Laura observed.

"To be honest, Aunty Laura, I'm in a bit of a quandary," Maisie admitted. "I really don't know what to do and I could do with some help."

"That sounds ominous. What's the problem, Maisie?" Laura asked curiously.

"It's Damon, well no, it's me," Maisie began. "I don't know what to say. I've been chatting to Mum and she says it's my decision and mine alone."

"What decision? Laura asked.

"Sorry, I'm not making much sense am I," Maisie confessed.

"Let's start again shall we?" said Laura laughing "hello Maisie, how are you?"

"I've got a bit of a problem and I need some help" Maisie repeated, now feeling a little easier. "Damon wants me to move to Kefalos permanently," she told Laura.

"And why is that a problem?" Laura questioned.

"I'm not sure if I can agree to it," Maisie told her.

"Why is that, Darling?" Laura further questioned.

"I'm not sure I can leave Mum and Dad," she said with honesty, and then went on to tell her auntie, "But Mum says it's up to me. It's my decision."

"Okay, apart from Mum and Dad, what objections do you have to moving out to Kefalos?" Laura queried, but Maisie remained silent. "Are you okay?" a worried Laura asked.

"Yes," Maisie replied. "Aunty Laura, it's a big step for me to take and I'm not sure I have the confidence to do it."

"Well I did it, and I was also very vulnerable at the time." Laura reminded her. "It was the best thing I ever did. Just look at what I have now, a lovely husband and two beautiful children I never thought I'd have."

"So Aunty Laura, what do you think I should do?" Laura pleaded.

"As your mum said, it's your decision, but you need to have faith in yourself and don't make any snap decisions. Think about it and think it through. Think about what's best for you and what is best for baby Alexander."

"I've been thinking about this for days now, Aunty, but I just don't know what to do," Maisie claimed again.

"Do you love Damon?" Laura questioned.

"Yes," Laura answered, without any hesitation.

"Do you want to marry Damon?" Laura continued.

"I think so," Maisie muttered, but then changed her reply to, "Yes, I want to marry him."

"Maisie, do you love Damon enough to move to Kefalos to be with him? We would all love to have you here with us, but only if you could be happy. Will you be happy living here with us?" Laura heard Maisie sigh on the other end of the phone.

"Thank you, Auntie Laura," Maisie reacted. "I think I can see things a little clearer now. I'll let you know when I decide what I'll do. You've helped me a lot. Thanks again."

"Anytime sweetheart," Laura said ending the call.

As Maisie put her phone down she felt like things seemed a little clearer now, but she thought perhaps it would be a good idea to ask her sister, Mia, whilst Laura's words were still fresh in her mind.

"Parakalo," Mia said as she answered the phone to Maisie's call.

"Oh don't you start that Greek stuff, that's the same greeting I received from Auntie Laura," Maisie laughed. "Hi Mia, its Maisie, how are you?"

After the niceties were exchanged, Maisie explained the problem she was phoning about and told Mia about the conversation she'd just had with Aunty Laura. Mia listened intently, considered Maisie's options, and then gave her opinion.

"Well Sis, if you have phoned to ask what I think you should do, I would say do it. Come and move here tomorrow," she laughed. "It was all I ever wanted, once I'd been to Kefalos, and I am so happy here that I feel blessed every day."

"What about Mum and Dad?" Maisie asked.

"What you mean?" Mia questioned

"I would be leaving them on their own," Maisie said guiltily.

"Are they old and infirm?" Mia asked.

"Not at all, but the stables are hard work," she pointed out to her sister.

"They could employ someone to help them," Mia countered. "It's not like they're poor!"

"When you put it like that," Maisie laughed.

"So Maisie, when are you coming?" Mia jumped in, but still sensed reluctance on her sister's part, so she continued. "Look Sis, Damon wants to marry you and that's a fabulous excuse for a party!"

"What about Mum and Dad?" Maisie questioned again.

"Look Maisie, I think you're using Mum and Dad for an excuse, not a reason for not coming to live here with Damon," Mia interrogated.

"I'm not," Maisie retaliated. "Honestly I'm not."

"Mum and Dad can come out to visit whenever they like and we'd all be together. Maybe they might even retire here themselves when the time comes." Mia could practically hear Maisie thinking about this, so she went in for the biggie!

"If you really want my advice, ring Damon now and get things moving. Tell him 'Yes-Yes-Yes' and let's get the ball rolling. I promise, you will never regret moving to Kefalos, and that's a 'little pinkie finger' promise."

Maisie couldn't help but laugh at her sister; she was so full of the joys of life. Perhaps that was what life in Kefalos does for you. She decided she must ring Damon, but first she needed to speak with her mum.

Suzie was so pleased that her daughter had made the decision to move to Kefalos. Although she would miss her and Alexander, she also knew that Maisie and the little one would be happy there.

"You'd better let Damon know your decision," she advised her daughter. "You never know, he may have changed his mind and found someone else to marry!" Suzie joked. They both laughed at this.

At that very moment, Alexander woke from his nap and let them know, in true Greek fashion, that he was hungry.

"Well my darling baby, it looks like we're going on a big adventure," Maisie said to her little boy a few minutes later. "Mummy has a lot of packing to do."

After she'd fed and changed Alexander, she picked up the phone, took a deep breath and phoned Damon. She hoped he would answer promptly, because she didn't want to lose her nerve and change her mind.

"Hi Maisie," he said, recognising the number. "Is anything wrong?"

"Should there be?" she answered nervously.

"Well you don't usually call me when I'm working," he reminded her.

"Sorry, is it a bad time?" she queried.

"Well my coffee may get cold, but I guess I can spare you a few moments," he joked. "What do you want?"

"You!" she replied.

"Me? Okay," he questioned curiously.

"I want to be with you," she revealed.

"Okay," he said again, still confused. "I miss you too."

"No," she demanded. "I want to be with you, all the time. I want to be with you permanently, in Kefalos," she admitted.

"Do you want to come and visit?" Damon asked, trying to make sense of what she was saying.

"No," she gushed. "Listen very carefully to what I'm saying. I want to come with Alexander and live with you there in Kefalos, and to be with you forever."

"You mean you want to come here and............"

"Yes," Maisie butted in. "I want to come to Kefalos and marry you, and be with you forever as a family. That is if you still want to marry me?"

Damon couldn't believe what he was hearing. Maisie could practically hear his brain whirring with all the thoughts running through it.

"Well then, you'd better start packing," Damon finally said. "I'll get a flight as soon as I can and we'll sort everything."

"You sound as enthusiastic as my sister," Maisie told him happily.

"Maisie, this is my dream coming true," Damon replied, and she could hear the joy in his voice. This made her feel very happy and relieved, as the decision she'd just made was probably the biggest decision she'd ever made in her life!

Damon flew back to England a few days later to 'Strike while the iron is hot.' He didn't want to give Maisie time to change her mind.

She couldn't believe how excited she was to see Damon. It was just like being a teenager again in the first throes of a love affair. He was just as excited and delighted to see Maisie. He hugged and kissed her so much he never wanted to let her go. He then picked up Alexander and hugged and kissed him also. The baby first put up a bit of a resistance, but then gurgled and smiled at Daddy.

Very quickly, everything was organised and they were ready to begin their new lives together in Kefalos. Sad goodbyes were said to Maisie's mum and dad, with promises to ring when they arrived safely. They also promised to call Suzie to let her know as soon as possible about the wedding plans, so that she and Dad could arrange cover at the stables and organise flights to Kos.

The moment had now come to drive away from her present home and the memories it contained and begin a new stage of her life with the man she knew she loved, hoping that she was giving her son the best possible lifestyle.

As they boarded the plane at Manchester Airport, Maisie cradled Alexander in one arm and Damon held her free hand. He knew this was difficult for her leaving her parents behind. It would be slightly easier for him, as he'd been away from his parents before and was now actually returning to his true home.

This time it was Mia who came to collect them upon arrival at the airport in Kos. She'd borrowed Laura's people carrier to make sure all the luggage would fit easily inside the vehicle, since she only had a very small car. When all were safely inside they began the familiar journey from the airport to Kefalos.

Mia was so happy to see her sister, and particularly happy to see her baby boy. She'd found immense happiness here in Kefalos and was sure Maisie would too.

Damon gave Mia directions to his home in the village and she carefully navigated the narrow streets, finally arriving safely at their new island home.

Maisie remembered the last time she'd been here and how their love making in this house had now changed their lives forever. They were no longer a couple, but were now a family of three.

Damon quickly put Alexander's cot together and the baby soon took advantage of it. Almost immediately, he was sleeping soundly.

"Well, the baby's sleeping," Damon announced. "Would you care to take advantage of our sleeping arrangements?"

"Why Sir, I really don't know what you mean," Maisie laughed, speaking in an exaggerated Southern Bell drawl.

"Madame, I do believe you do," Damon replied. He held out his hand which Maisie took, and with a huge smile on her face, he led her to the bedroom.

The next morning, being Sunday, it was always a family day. Mia had told them they were all invited to Laura's house in the afternoon for a family get together, and as a 'Welcome to Kefalos' party. They had thanked Mia for the invitation and said they'd be thrilled to be there and meet all the family.

It was getting quite late in the evening now, so totally exhausted by the day's travel, Maisie put Alexander down and kissed him goodnight He looked so content in his new cot; he looked super happy.

She turned to find Damon gazing at her. "You are a fantastic mother," he whispered and she smiled at him. "And you are a beautiful and very desirable woman," he added. "And I desire you, again."

"What, again," she mocked. He took her hand and kissed it, leaving no doubt in her mind what it was that he wanted. "It must be something to do with the Kefalos air," she remarked smiling.

It had been a long day and an even longer wait for Damon to have Maisie and Alexander here in Kefalos, but they were here now and he didn't want to waste a second. Quietly they made their way to the bedroom again, gently undressed each other and climbed into bed.

"I still cannot believe you are here," Damon murmured quietly, so as not to disturb Alexander.

"Nor me," she replied. "I seem to remember, though it seems like a lifetime ago, you brought me here before and, well, you know what you did."

"Yes I remember," he smiled.

"Do it again," she pleaded and he smiled

He loved Maisie so much. Soon they would be officially married, but to all intents and purposes she was already his wife. Just how lucky could one man be? They made soft and gentle love, and it was wonderful.

Now here they were again, planning yet another wedding in Kefalos. Almost all the families seemed to be involved in one way or another.

James and Caitlin were very busy at the paediatric centre and apologised because they couldn't help a great deal, but agreed that Damon's mother and father could stay at their villa for the two weeks they were coming out for the wedding.

Nikos, after much discussion with Damon and Maisie, had agreed that the reception could be held around his and Laura's pool at the villa.

Mia went to Athens with Maisie to buy a wedding dress for her and a bridesmaid dress for herself. It was good to spend quality time with her sister, and also learn much of the ins and outs of Kefalos life.

It was also nice to have time away from their roles as parents. This was a benefit of Greek life, where grandparents usually cared for the children. Here it was mostly down to Laura, Toula and Sophia to take care of baby Alexander, and they did it willingly.

Maisie and Damon were to be married in the big church situated half way up the hill towards Kefalos village, with the paved area at the rear of the church providing a perfect backdrop, with its panoramic view of the Bay of Kamari. Chairs were placed on the paved area behind the church, and a black wrought iron arch was positioned in front of these seats.

As the guests arrived, Dimitris and James escorted them to their allotted place. Damon's parents sat on the front row on the right and Suzie sat on the left, proudly holding Alexander in her arms.

The traditional Greek ceremony was performed by the village priest, who'd also agreed to carry out the baptism of Alexander at the end of the marriage ceremony.

The girls at the stables had arranged to borrow a vintage cart from friends, which they'd decorated with flowers and had hitched it to one of the horses, so Maisie and her father, Daniel, arrived at the church in fine style. It would also return Maisie and her new husband to the reception at the villa after the service.

The bride looked beautiful in a full length gown with a train trailing behind. She'd chosen pale pink, as she felt white was a little inappropriate as she was already a mother. She wore a headband of pearls, which held back her long dark hair.

Damon was immensely proud to be marrying Maisie. His Greek friends, who were waiting on the road outside the church, clapped and cheered when they left.

A lively and noisy celebration took place later at the villa, where the wine and ouzo flowed generously.

Later in the evening the happy couple departed, complete with their sleeping son, leaving the revellers to carry on with the festivities.

The drinking and the dancing continued long into the night and through to the early hours of the morning. It became a party which would be spoken about for many years in the future.

CHAPTER 16
AN UNEXPECTED CALL

It certainly wasn't the phone call Maisie had been expecting, but one she'd actually been dreading. When she heard the words coming from her mother's mouth, her feelings of guilt were totally all consuming.

"I am sorry to tell you, my darling, but your father has suddenly passed away," Suzie told her with a shaky voice. Maisie couldn't believe it. It was only a few months since he'd been there to give her away at the wedding.

Tears streamed down her face as she tried to find the words she wanted to say, eventually replying, "Oh Mum, I'm so sorry. I don't know what to say."

"There's nothing to say, my darling, no one expected this or had any clue it was about to happen," Mum reassured her. "I have to tell Mia. I tried to call her but couldn't get through."

"Do you want me to tell her?" Maisie asked

"No, I should do it," her mother stressed. "But please could you tell James and Laura for me?"

They chatted for little while and Maisie told Suzie she would get to England as soon as possible. "If you need to talk, Mum, call me. I am always here for you," she promised.

After the call had ended, Maisie stood completely stunned after hearing what she'd just been told. A few minutes later the phone rang again. This time it was Mia. She was absolutely bereft after hearing the news about her father. She also promised to get to England as soon as possible.

"We should go together," she suggested to Maisie.

"Of course," Maisie agreed, and they arranged to get together to plan the journey.

Maisie phoned the rest of the family. James and Laura were both saddened by the news, shocked to hear of the sudden death of their brother in law.

It was impossible for James to take any time away from the centre, but Aunty Laura said she would go with the girls and a few days later, they touched down in a very rainy Manchester.

On a dark and cloudy winter's day, Daniel, Suzie's husband of many years, father to Mia and Maisie and brother in law to Laura and James, was laid to rest.

The funeral was a quiet affair, a small family gathering followed by a meal at a local restaurant with the family from Daniel's side.

Maisie was still feeling guilty about her father's death. Had his death been connected in any way to her decision to leave them and move to Kefalos? She told her mother of her feelings.

"Of course it wasn't your fault, Maisie," Suzie revealed. "Your father was very happy when you left to marry Damon, and he could not have been prouder the day he gave you away."

"But I always felt guilty," Maisie admitted.

"Well don't!" Suzie ordered. "We both knew you would not be here with us forever. You had your own life to lead."

"Mum, why don't you sell the stables and come to Kefalos and join the family?" Maisie suggested.

"Dad and I had already talked about selling the business," Suzie smiled.

Hearing this really shocked Maisie, but she was even more shocked when her mother revealed that she and her father had already negotiated the sale of the riding school.

"The sale was organised a while ago," Suzie revealed, stunning her daughter. "Dad and I have been looking for a small flat to move into, but we haven't found anything yet. But now of course it's too late."

"Too late for Dad, but not for you," Maisie insisted.

"Maybe," Suzie offered quietly.

"Look Mum, why don't you come back with us for a week or two, so we can all be together?" Maisie suggested. "You could spend time with your grandchildren, and the milder weather would be good for you, much better than this damp murky weather here."

Suzie tried to offer a few negatives, but every negative from her was counteracted by many positives from the girls. In the end, she had to concede.

"You can stay at Granny's house, the one she built with Granddad, the house by the beautiful cove," Maisie said.

"You can stay there for as long as you like," Mia chipped in.

"Okay, okay, I give in!" Suzie laughed. "The stables have been transferred and the new owner is ready to take over immediately, so there's nothing stopping me now."

As soon as all the legal and financial dealings had been finalised, the girls and their mother, Suzie, took the flight to Athens and then transferred to a flight bound for Kos.

Suzie was happy to stay at Jenny's house at the Cove. She'd stayed there on numerous summer holidays with the girls' father, Daniel.

"Maisie, would you mind staying with me for the first few days?" she asked her daughter.

"Of course I will, Mum," she replied. "And I'll bring baby Alexander with me." This made her mother very happy.

At first, Suzie still seemed intent on finding a little flat back in England, but as the days and weeks passed she talked less and less about it and more about how she enjoyed being here with her brother and sister, children, and grandchildren.

All the family equally enjoyed having Suzie here on the island with them.

"Look Mum," Maisie said one afternoon. "There's no need for you to rush back to England. Why don't you at least stay here for the winter and avoid all the cold, damp weather. You can stay here in this house as long as you want. After all, it's as much your house as it is for any one of us."

Suzie had never thought about it this way, and it did make sense to stay and enjoy some winter warmth. She also loved playing her role as Grandma, as well as going to the stables with Maisie and Damon and helping out with their horses.

Following the Christmas festivities, Suzie told everyone that she was very happy living in the house on her own and never felt lonely, as she felt close to her mum, Jenny when staying there. She also had happy memories of her time spent here with Mia and Maisie's father. Because of this, the two girls decided they would spend less time with their mum and allow her to build an island life of her own.

Over the past few weeks, Suzie had met and befriended a male friend, another widower, who lived just outside the village. She and Lukas frequently met for coffee or went for walks together, he even persuaded Suzie to go swimming in the sea. Although the water was still very cold, freezing in fact, but once she was in it made her feel both alive and invigorated.

Mia and Maisie were delighted their mother had met this lovely man and she was now far less dependent on them. It made things far easier for everyone all round.

After enjoying a very happy winter, as spring approached, Suzie spoke to James about the house. "Look James, I have to ask you something a little embarrassing," she began.

"What on earth could that be?" James questioned.

"If I decide to stay on the island, would you mind if my friend Lukas moved in with me?" she asked coyly.

"Of course not, Sis," he smiled. "We've all been secretly hoping that you would find a nice man who would give you a reason to stay here with us."

"What about Laura?" Suzie questioned tentatively.

"Especially Laura," James laughed.

A little later that day, Suzie asked the same question of her daughters and was surprised by their answers.

"We both know that you loved Dad, but he's gone," Mia said stating the facts.

"You're still relatively young, Mum," Maisie offered, "so you deserve to enjoy the rest of your life. If Lukas makes you happy, then we are all happy."

"Thank you girls," a relieved Suzie replied smiling.

"We love you, Mum," they said in unison.

"I love you too," Suzie smiled.

"Besides," Maisie laughed, "instant baby sitter!"

During a family get together, Suzie made an official announcement. "Firstly can I say how happy I have been, staying here with you all for the past few months?"

Everyone stopped to look at her, wondering what she was about to say.

"As you know, I have been thinking about returning to England for a long time, but I now know that all the reasons for my returning, no longer exist," she smiled at them all as she continued. "If I returned to England, I would be there all on my own, but here I am surrounded by family, and Lukas." She looked at her Greek boyfriend, smiled, and he smiled back at her in return. "I never believed I would ever consider living here on Kos, but like all of you, I have caught the Kefalos bug."

Everyone laughed when hearing this. They all knew exactly what it was she meant.

"Like my mother and my children's grandmother, Jenny, tragedy has brought me here, but if I have even half the life she had after moving here, then I will be a very lucky girl indeed."

"Come on, Suzie," James interrupted. "So are you staying with us or not?"

"Yes," Suzie replied. "You can now consider me as a resident of Kefalos. I know I will be very happy here and have a fabulous rest of my life. It's written in the stars."

CHAPTER 17
LAURA

In all the years since she'd lived there, Laura had never seen the sea so calm on this side of the island. Kochylari was renowned for its fabulous waves, yet today the sea was like mirrored glass, apart from the occasional ripple, it was more like a large lake.

The sky today was a beautiful blue, with just a few wispy clouds dotted here and there. Across from the beach, the island of Kalymnos was so clear you could pick out all the buildings surrounding the harbour, along with the craggy mountains soaring above.

As the children, Dimitris and Toula waded into the sea; Laura looked on as their bodies were reflected in the still water. Her two children had now become adults, and soon they would be having children of their own.

After their swim, they sat on the shore to dry off in the sun before returning to the villa, where as always on a Sunday, a traditional family meal would be waiting for them.

It was the Greek way, for family was everything and their together time was precious. Sundays were a time to get together to talk about times past and remember family members who were no longer with them. It was also the time for planning new adventures, or just to sit together as a family.

As Laura had been watching them frolic in the waves that afternoon, she thought back to when they'd first been born.

After she'd suffered a horrible miscarriage, she was surprised to find she was pregnant with Dimitris. Laura and her husband, Nikos, were so delighted at the prospect of being parents, and their happiness was made complete when Toula was born soon after.

Dimitris, the elder child of Laura and Nikos had learned to sail with his father from a very early age. He mastered sailing techniques and learned to read potential problems with the weather and tides.

Dimitris knew one day he would inherit his father's empire, having taken over the running of the company to allow his father to enjoy his retirement. He also knew it would be hard for his father to relinquish control of his beloved company, but that was way in the future.

He'd had a happy childhood. He enjoyed school and had lots of friends in the village, and was always involved in all the various activities, one of the main ones being the annual blessing of the waters.

The Greek Orthodox Church celebrates the blessing of the waters during epiphany, and during the ceremony, 'the 'dive of the Cross' takes place.

The priest throws the cross into the water as a symbolic gesture to bless the sea. The lucky person who retrieves the cross is considered to be blessed all through the year.

The ritual throwing of the cross is believed to give the water the powers to cleanse and sanitise. Despite icy cold temperatures of the sea, this ceremony normally takes place every year on 'Twelfth Night,' the 6th of January.

The annual day of the diving for the cross in Kefalos had arrived. All the villagers congregated on the harbour wall waiting for the priest to throw the cross into the water so the fun could begin. All the young men and boys stood poised in anticipation. As the cross was thrown in, each of them dived at the same time and started to swim beneath the waves looking for the prized possession. It was a great honour to be the one who found it and held it aloft.

Today it was Dimitris who retrieved it. He held the cross up high so all could see that he had it, but as he did so, he noticed one of the younger lads hadn't surfaced from the dive. He quickly relinquished the cross and gave it to a fellow swimmer and then dived deep underwater again to search for the missing boy. Not finding him, he resurfaced for air and dived again.

It was then he saw the young boy madly flapping about in the deeper water. He'd caught himself on a length of wire and was being held by his foot, unable to release it. Dimitris surfaced for an extra large breath and dived again.

The boy was now panicking and reached out trying to grab Dimitris. He managed to hold him off whilst he released the boys foot from the wire. Many people were watching from the harbour walls, and luckily, Dimitris was possibly one of the finest swimmers, or divers they knew.

The two boys surfaced together, the young boy coughing and choking as he was dragged from the water. A cheer went up from the watching crowd and the priest gave Dimitris an extra special blessing.

Luckily his Uncle James was on hand to check the other boy and it was declared he hadn't taken in too much water, so no real damage had been done. He was really lucky that Dimitris had noticed his absence when the cross was raised.

Dimitris was the hero of the day, with the story of the rescue being told over and over again in the village, making both Laura and Nikos extremely proud of their son.

By the age of eighteen, Dimitris was employed by his father's company, having already worked hard to prove to his father that he had the skills and knowledge to work with him. He'd grown into a tall and attractive man, being the mirror image of his father in both looks and character.

He'd caught the eye of many young girls, both at home and the many places he visited for work. Besides his good looks, of course there was the fact the girls knew that one day he would become a very wealthy man, which made him a sought after, eligible bachelor. He was well liked and held in high esteem wherever he went.

He'd dated a few young girls, but as he was still young he decided he hadn't found love as yet, so was not ready to settle down.

He had a flat in Athens close to the office and near to the airport, so he could easily travel to wherever he was required to be. His job also allowed him to visit many countries dotted around the world.

Back in Kefalos he kept his room in the villa as a room to sleep in but had also converted it into an office, with all the equipment he needed to also work from home.

His younger sister, Toula, was the youngest child of Laura and Nikos. She was a pretty child and had developed into an attractive teenager. Like her brother, she also loved the sea and was always involved in community projects frequently, ones her father was sponsoring.

She had a good head on her shoulders and knew what she wanted from life, and was intent on following a career quite different from that of her brother. Because she was so impressed with the work of her Uncle James, she'd decided from a young age that she too wanted to be a doctor.

After working hard at school, Toula secured a place in Manchester, at the very same medical school her Uncle James had attended years before. She would live in a shared flat quite close to her Auntie Suzie for her years of study.

She'd been brought up to speak both Greek and English, so she had no fears of living in a foreign country. She knew that once she'd completed her studies and gained her qualifications, a position awaited her in the paediatric centre in Kefalos.

She would miss being able to take a morning dip in the sea or lazing on the beautiful sandy beaches of the island, but would most of all miss being with her cousins and the rest of the family. However, she knew that the time would quickly pass and she'd still be able to return for holidays.

At the end of her course, Toula returned to Kos as a qualified doctor, taking her position at the centre her father had financed and her uncle managed.

Nikos, like every Greek father was expected to provide a home for his daughter. Whilst she was in England he purchased a plot of land not far from his own home and commissioned a house to be built in readiness for her return.

There had been no talk of her having anyone special in her life during phone calls and video chats made to the family, so there didn't seem to be any urgency about finishing the building, which would normally be completed in readiness for a daughter's wedding.

Toula had remained friends with her school mates from Kos and when she returned she reacquainted herself with them. Some of the girls had married and some were now mothers with children of their own. Other friends had fled the nest and moved to other countries, and a few were in long term relationships. However, a few were like Toula and did not have partners, being still single. It hadn't been on the high priority list for her to have someone special in her life, since she wanted to set herself up in a good career before contemplating settling down, and this was where she was now.

Laura loved her children so much. She was proud of the people they'd become and was thankful each and every day that she'd been lucky to find her husband, Nikos, and to be the mother of two wonderful offspring.

CHAPTER 18
AT SEASON'S END

Now, as October heralded the end of another season, with the evenings becoming a little chillier, cardigans were being worn again and coats became the order of the day. Although the sun could still be fierce during the daytime, after the sun went down the temperature would drop considerably.

The month of October also brought varying weather and sometimes it could be particularly inclement. There was a strange stillness in the air and a feeling of expectation that something was about to happen. Suddenly from nowhere a strong blast of wind came across the land, shaking and bending the swaying trees.

The black clouds began to roll in, a slight rumble could be heard, then began the terrific light show. Daggers of purple and silver light cascaded onto the parched earth below, which had seen no rain since the early months of the year. One moment saw the darkness of the black clouds and the next brought the bright light, as the lightning darted across the sky. It was spectacular.

Bars and cafes quickly pulled down their rain shields. Parasols and loungers were quickly brought away from the edge of the menacing sea, as tourists huddled in bars to shelter from the deluge.

People tended to chat in hushed tones with the volume of laughter and jollity muted, trying not to show any fear they had of this terrible force of nature.

Some holidaymakers were disappointed with the change in weather, looking to find reasons to be refunded for the lack of sunshine that day!

The Greeks knew it would soon pass and everywhere would be dry again, but they also knew that the frequency of these storms would increase towards the end of October and into November.

This marked the transition from the hustle and bustle of the summer season, changing to the more gentle and sedateness of the winter months.

For the local workers and business owners it was now time to rest, time to prepare for next year's holiday season, time to recharge their batteries, and time to spend with family and friends.

Almost every family had an olive grove somewhere in Kefalos, if not near their home it would be on land close by under the hills surrounding the village.

It became a real family affair when it was time to pick the olives, with everyone being involved. Jenny's extended family was no different, and those who were free and able to help, congregated in the family olive grove.

Nikos shouted out the orders and the family did as they were instructed. Large nets were placed under the trees to collect the valuable fruit. The older more experienced gatherers would use mechanical shakers, whist the younger members stripped the branches by hand. The children played in the olive groves while the parents and friends went on to collect the olives.

When the crop was picked, packed and sent to the factory, all the members of this family, along with the friends who'd helped them with the harvest went back to Nikos and Laura's villa, where food and wine was provided in abundance to celebrate a good harvest. A good party was enjoyed by all.

One of Laura's favourite times of the year had to be the festive holidays. An early sign that Christmas was coming to Kefalos was when the community officers started work putting up the street lights and decorations along the streets. Reindeers,

Santa figures and tinsel were hung from wire, and little huts appeared along the streets in preparation for the markets.

The run up to the season brought the Christmas markets to Kefalos. Tables laden with goodies were set up along the streets and also in the little huts, with many of the villagers making things to sell. The intention was to raise funds for the local school.

Many of the English residents would bake traditional Christmas food, such as Christmas cake, mince tarts and brandy snaps. The Greeks would make cookies and biscuits with cinnamon and almonds. The older women would crochet hats and scarves, or make patchwork quilts. Some of the more creatively inclined would make stuffed toys, or ornaments made from stones or driftwood. Some made decorated candles to burn on Christmas Eve at the traditional midnight mass.

As always, the community came together to make Christmas a special occasion for everyone. Families would gather together, and distant relatives from mainland Greece would come to spend time with them.

Children would perform in presentations at the school, and then impatiently await the arrival of Santa Claus.

This was how it was for the children of this English dynasty, the family who over the years had come to make Kefalos their home.

The biggest celebrations on the island were always at Easter. The family attended church together and burned decorated candles.

At midnight they celebrate with a firework display and also by throwing sticks of dynamite down the mountainside. Because of the shape of the bay and the mountains surrounding it, the noise of the explosions reverberated all around, with the houses shaking from the vibrations.

On Easter Sunday the family would gather to spit roast the traditional goat in the garden. This was one of the most important days in the Greek calendar. This year it was James's turn to host the event at his and Caitlin's home. The extended family of Jenny's children, Laura and Nikos, with their children Dimitris and Toula, Mia and Sophia, with Kali and Babis, James and Caitlin with Grace and Maisie, Damon and Alexander were all together at this noisy happy Greek family time.

And now spring was here, preparations began yet again for the coming tourist season in Kefalos. The smell of fresh paint filled the air. Hotel owners cut down unruly plants which had taken over the outside areas, whilst others removed the wrapping that had been wound around delicate palms to protect them from the winds and sea spray, during the winter months.

Cars which had been stored inside restaurant buildings were now brought outside, with the empty space being filled with newly painted chairs and tables, all now looking beautiful and fresh.

Swimming pools, green from being left untreated, were emptied with their slimy contents spilling down the roads. Leaves and branches piled high were stuffed into overflowing bins waiting for the next refuse collections.

The railings along the harbour road were rubbed down, removing the rust in readiness for painting, usually carried out after the start of the season.

Boards outside restaurants had fresh menus pinned to them. Volunteers began to clear the rubbish brought ashore by the high tides of winter in readiness for the bulldozers that would level off the uneven beaches, making them ready for the sun loungers and umbrellas to be replaced. It was a flurry of activity after the six months of the closed season.

This was the never ending cycle, year after year, with sleepy Kefalos coming out of hibernation again, ready for the coming visitors. These were the events which punctuated each and every passing year for all those who were lucky enough to call Kefalos their home.

CHAPTER 19
IN THEIR STARS

Every member of this extended family had been led to Kefalos by the stars, with it becoming home for them.

Jenny moved here to keep a promise she made to John, her dying husband. Although being alone for a while, she soon began to call Kefalos her home and settled into life in the village.

She felt that John was always here with her, and often, as he told her to, she would look to the stars and speak to him. He always listened.

Kefalos weaved its magic and she soon found love again with Yiannis. They were married at the little church on Kastri Island, spending their remaining years together in the home overlooking the cove which was special to them in many ways, especially as this was where she first met Yiannis many years ago, when she rescued him from the sea.

When Yiannis passed away he was buried in a plot overlooking the cove, and when Jenny died a few years later she was buried next to him. Together, side by side they would stay in Kefalos forever.

Jenny's daughter, Laura came to Kefalos to heal her broken heart when her partner betrayed her, sadly with her best friend at the time. She soon fell under the island's spell and decided to stay.

She met and married Nikos, and their marriage was blessed with the children they thought they could never have.

Then it was James who had fallen under its spell when he visited Kefalos and fell for its charms. With the help of Nikos they built a health centre, and although it was built with his brother in law's money, the locals all called it James and Caitlin's paediatric centre.

James had always told Caitlin that if it was in their stars it would happen, and for them – it did.

Suzie, the eldest daughter of John and Jenny was an English girl through and through. She'd never considered a move to the island until, like her mother, Jenny, her husband passed away. The family then made her see the sense of moving to Kefalos to be with the family, and she never looked back.

Suzie was happy for her daughter, Mia, when she found love with Sophia while working with Uncle James in Kefalos. Although unsure at first, it soon became apparent to Suzie that Mia and Sophia loved each other very much, and Suzie now adored her granddaughter, Kali, and grandson, Babis.

When her other daughter, Maisie had met a Greek boy from Kefalos who wanted her to move out there with him, it was inevitable it would happen, and it did. She and her son, Alexander, moved to Kefalos to marry and live with Damon.

Kefalos had healed family wounds and helped them find love. It had taught them that anything was possible, that there was always hope and that most problems could be overcome. This was a place where love could be found in the most unlikely situations, and that family was the most important thing in life.

As they all sat around the dining table enjoying the Sunday gathering at hers and Nikos's home, Laura looked around at all the family seated there enjoying each other's company. She smiled to herself as she thought that all this was thanks to one woman, her mother, Jenny. She was the reason for them all living here, and without her, none of this dynasty would have ever existed.

"I would like to say something," Laura suddenly announced whilst standing. Everyone stopped to look at her. "I would like to propose a toast to the wonderful woman who followed her dreams, a woman without whom none of us would be here today. Please stand and raise your glasses."

All the family, although unsure of what Laura was about to say, stood anyway and waited for her to continue.

To Jenny," Laura began, "God bless you, Mum, and thank you for giving us this wonderful life here in Kefalos, on the beautiful island of Kos."

"To Jenny," all the family toasted.

"Thank you Jenny, thank you Mum, thank you for following your convictions and beliefs, and thank you most for believing what Dad once said about looking to the stars," she said this with tears in her eyes, but they were tears of joy.

As she sat down, Laura again looked at her family sitting together and enjoying life. She felt blessed. She was happy that they'd all seen sense to follow their dreams and believe what was written in their stars.

THE END

(PTO)

MORE BOOKS IN THE TRILOGY

LOOK TO THE STARS
(Book 1)

"Whenever you feel sad or alone, look to the stars and I will be there for you. I'll be with you forever." - These were the last words ever spoken to Jenny by her husband, John, as he lay on his deathbed. Moments later he died in her arms. This is her story.

Jenny is a lovely teenage girl from a wonderful family, who along with her best friend, Sue, has an enjoyment for life. This normally involves going to meet friends at 'Bob's Café,' along with meeting boys, socializing and having fun.

Both girls have a 'Sliding Doors' moment when Jenny goes on holiday with her family to Cornwall, whilst Sue goes to Mallorca. Something happens to both girls during these holidays which will change their lives forever. Life for them will never be the same again.

WHEN THE STARS ALIGN
(Book 2 – Laura's Story)

This follow up book is the story of Jenny and John's youngest child, their daughter, Laura.

Laura's life turns sour when she discovers that the man whom she thinks is the love of her life has been having an affair with a girl she thought of as her best friend.

In an attempt to get over the failed relationship, she goes to Kefalos to be close to Jenny and hopes the island can heal her as is did her mum all those years ago.

This is a delightful story of love and loss, a mixture of light and dark that will have you in tears of sadness one minute, whilst the next you will be crying with joy.

If you know the island of Kos and particularly the area of Kefalos, then every page will leap out at you and transport you to the wonderful Greek sunshine.

(All three books are available as both eBooks and Paperbacks at your local Amazon site)

Printed in Great Britain
by Amazon